COULD RICKY GIVE HIM AWAY? A TWO-YEAR-OLD?

He couldn't take chances. "Wed wabbit!" Ricky had said. He said a lot of things real clear for a little kid.

He couldn't be careless. Never again. He had to keep up with the stories in the paper, know what the cops were doing and who they thought they were looking for.

The only other person who might have seen him following Lorna was that old bag lady with her shopping cart full of rags. Surely the cops wouldn't believe anything she said. Even at a distance he'd been able to see that the old hag was nuts....

★

"Johnston's ability to create a chilly mood is not something that will be easily shaken."
—*Atlanta Magazine*

JANE JOHNSTON

PRAY FOR RICKY FOSTER

TORONTO · NEW YORK · LONDON · PARIS
AMSTERDAM · STOCKHOLM · HAMBURG
ATHENS · MILAN · TOKYO · SYDNEY

PRAY FOR RICKY FOSTER

A Worldwide Mystery/March 1991

First published by St. Martin's Press Incorporated.

ISBN 0-373-26068-7

To Pete

ONE

LORNA LOOKED AROUND. She did not see the man in the blue sweatsuit. Her fear did not lessen.

The old, buried nightmare was stirring.

Falling leaves splattered the sidewalk on a sudden gust of wind. The little boy, sitting in the old man's lap, looked over at her with alarm in his soft, brown eyes. The day had been sultry, thick with remembered summer, but now the sky was heavy and a sharp wind had risen.

She and Ricky had stayed too long in the park.

Harold Bloor squinted at the sky through nearsighted eyes. His veined hand fumbled for the switch that turned on his electric wheelchair. Ricky, forgetting his fear, squealed with joy.

"Last ride!" the old man cried. He turned the chair in a tight circle. "This is the way we take a ride, take a ride," he sang in a quavering voice. Ricky wrapped his little arms around Harold Bloor's neck and sang accompaniment in a tuneless treble.

Lorna glanced at the sky. She could no longer conceal her anxiety. She wanted to get Ricky home. It was hard to leave the old man. He took so much pleasure in their company. Poor old soul, so frail and lonely. He had so little to enjoy but the hours she and Ricky spent with him.

When the ride was over, she untangled Ricky from Harold Bloor's arms and settled him firmly into the stroller.

"Fuck!" said Ricky. The old man chuckled. Ricky leaned over and strained to reach the red plastic truck on the sidewalk. "Get fuck, Worna!" he demanded.

She picked up the toy and tucked it in beside him. "Say 'truck,' Ricky."

"Wed fuck," said Ricky with great satisfaction. One small arm clutched a piece of blanket that, when new, had been blue and velvety. Now it was gray and threadbare from many launderings. He rubbed his eyes, smudging a face already sticky from his afternoon juice.

"Say goodbye to Mr. Bloor, Ricky!"

Ricky waved a grubby fist. "Bye, Mister Boo!"

"Goodbye, Ricky, goodbye, Miss Meyers. Hurry home before it rains. I've kept you too long, and you've got farther to go than I do." The wheelchair hummed now as the old man headed toward the East Side.

Lorna slung her bag over her shoulder and set off quickly in the other direction. Runners, roller skaters, cyclists, parents with children in carriages and strollers, all scattered as the wind flung a fresh rush of leaves and the first stinging drips. Added to her dread of getting caught in the rain was the mindless, meaningless fear.

The man in the blue sweatsuit. She had not seen him for a week.

There was a sudden squeal of rusty wheels. Lorna quickly drew the stroller off the sidewalk onto the grass.

"Fucking bitch! Outta my way!" Bloodshot eyes peered at her from under a fringe of matted gray hair. The old woman's skin was an indeterminate shade of gray. She might be black, she might be white. Her shapeless form was layered in sad, filthy garments topped by a heavy coat, stiff with dirt and fastened in the front with safety pins. Her swollen feet were thrust into a pair of worn sneakers many times too large.

Lorna had seen the old woman many times, but never this close. The witchlike figure, shuffling along behind a deep shopping cart filled with rags and papers, haunted this part of the park.

The woman's baleful glance swept Lorna from head to toe, then fastened on the sleeping child. She leaned over him. Her furious old face softened. "Look at the little lamb," she crooned. "Sleeping so sweet!" One grimy, clawlike hand reached out toward the child's soft cheek.

Ricky's head drooped over his blanket. If he woke up suddenly and saw the old woman's face so close to his, he would scream. Lorna pulled the stroller back.

"Bitch!" The bag lady glared. Her eyes were bright with hatred. "You're not fit to take care of him. I'll tell them what you are. They'll come and take him away from you!'' She gripped the handle of her cart and set it into squealing motion as purposefully as Lorna pushed the stroller.

When the woman had passed with a final, muttered curse, Lorna found that she was shaking. The old woman had always seemed merely pathetic, a sad outcast of the city.

Today even she was sinister.

At the edge of the drive, Lorna waited for the light to change. A straggle of runners pounded by. With the Marathon only a week away, the park was full of them, glassy-eyed, straining, intent, oblivious even to the rain which was coming down hard now. Lorna looked at them quickly. Green, gray, red—no blue suit among them.

Maybe he would not come back.

A week ago. That was the first time. She'd been sitting on one of the park benches. Mr. Bloor's wheelchair was drawn up near her. The old man had rambled on about his weak heart and his useless legs while Ricky noisily shoved his truck into a pile of leaves and twigs on the sidewalk.

The man in the blue suit had jogged by, one runner among many that day. She remembered him because he slowed down as he skirted the child in his path. He shot a quick glance at her. He had a red bandanna wound like a sweatband around his head of thick, dark hair, and the lower part of his face was hidden by a heavy beard. His eyes were invisible behind dark glasses.

A few days later he'd come back.

This time he sat down on a bench across from them. He was breathing fast, as if he needed time to catch his breath. But behind the dark lenses, she sensed his eyes were on her. She kept her face turned toward Mr. Bloor, and for once she was thankful for the old man's garrulity. She smiled and nodded at him, but all the while she was aware of that silent scrutiny from the man on the bench.

She felt an enormous relief when he got to his feet and padded away.

Two days later she and Ricky were watching a ball game from behind the chain-link fence that surrounded the playing field.

Behind her she heard footsteps on the grass. "Hello, there."
The voice was low and husky.

Startled, she turned to find him standing beside her. He was
taller than she remembered, six feet at least, and bulky rather
than fat. His heavy muscularity was emphasized by the soft
fabric of the blue sweatsuit.

The eyes behind the glasses met hers quickly, slyly, then
dropped to the child beside her. He squatted down beside the
little boy. "That's a real nice truck you got there, kid."

Ricky, shy with strangers, buried his face in his blanket.

The man rolled the red bandanna off his head. He unrolled
it, then deftly knotted it into a puppet. He thrust his hand into
it and waggled it in front of Ricky's buried face. "This rabbit
wants to see you," he sang.

Ricky peeped. Then, all shyness gone, he reached, giggling,
and cried, "Wabbit!"

"What color's the rabbit?"

"Wed!"

"Tell the rabbit your name," he coaxed.

The little boy was all smiles. "Wicky!" he said proudly.

"I'm Larry. Can you say Larry?"

"Warry?"

The man grinned. His mouth in the thick beard opened and
showed a row of small, even, almost childlike teeth. Lorna felt
a spasm of dislike. Something about this man sickened her,
brought nausea to her stomach and sweat to her face.

The man directed his question to Ricky, but his eyes were on
Lorna. "Bet you can't tell me her name!"

Before Ricky could open his mouth to say "Worna," she had
picked him up and jammed his legs into the stroller. "Time to
go, Ricky," she said quickly. "Mister Boo will wonder where
we are."

Ricky began to protest. "No! No go!"

Unheeding, she bumped the stroller roughly over the grass.
She had to get away. Dislike of this man had turned into fear.

Behind them the husky voice called out, "I'll show you the
rabbit again sometime, Ricky—and ducks and elephants!"

"Bye, Warry!" Ricky twisted around to wave.

She had not seen the man since then. But from that moment, the old sick shame had awakened, the shame she thought she had left behind, like her childhood, in the gray, terrible days when first Daddy and then Mom had died. And Linda, the older sister she adored, had become a grown-up overnight, too hardworking and too anxious to be bothered.

Ten years ago. Nine since Daddy died. Then Mom.

The past was behind her. She had to remember that. She was forgiven. She'd prayed for forgiveness—with tears rolling down her face and her whole body one terrible hurt.

Now she had a new life. She went to classes in the morning, and in the afternoons she looked after Ricky. He was such a good little boy. And Pat was so grateful that Lorna took care of him for five hours every day while she was in her studio painting.

Ricky's eyes were still closed. Not even the rain disturbed him. Lorna stopped to pull the blanket more snugly around him. She was shivering. Her corduroy jacket and denim skirt were becoming uncomfortably damp. Only a few more blocks to go—out of the park and down Central Park West to 92nd Street, where Pat and Rowland Foster lived on the top two floors of a brownstone. Under the trees that lined the park side of the avenue, the rain would not hit them so hard.

The sidewalk dipped into a hollow where the trees almost met overhead, forming a tunnel of wilting autumn foliage.

Lorna was suddenly struck by the silence. This spot had never seemed so lonely on sunny days when she could hear all around her the sounds of the park—the shrieks and squeals of children on the playground where she and Ricky spent part of every afternoon, the crack of a bat against a ball and the yells of the players just the other side of the thick hedge that crowded against the fence.

Now she heard only the patter of rain on the leaves over her head and the muted swish of hidden traffic winding through the park on 96th Street. The parents and sitters had hurried the children home. The ballplayers were silently intent on finishing the inning before rain ended their game.

Even the homeless old woman, who had gone ahead of her on the sidewalk, was nowhere in sight. She had disappeared, cart and all, into some hiding place, like an animal seeking shelter.

Lorna reached the place where, even on sunny days, she always hurried. At the bottom of the hollow, the sidewalk wound past the fire-blackened shell of a comfort station long ago abandoned to time and vandals. Most of its charred roof beams had fallen in and lay criss-crossed on the floor where weeds and saplings thrust themselves brutally through the broken tiles. Yellowing creepers wreathed the blind, empty windows. A sour stench of dead ashes and foul, rotting things stained the wet air.

Lorna gripped the handle of the stroller and quickened her steps. Not far now.

Footsteps behind her.

"Lorna? Don't you remember me?" His husky voice was soft and pleading.

She remembered.

TWO

SHE LAY splayed against the cracked, filthy tiles. Her eyes bulged, staring. They accused.

He choked and retched. His whole body was a spasm of sickness and anguish. "I didn't want to kill you, Lorna! I love you!"

No answer. Nothing but that silent, horrible stare. "You made me kill you, Lorna. You know that, don't you? You should have let me—"

Silence.

He got to his feet somehow and pulled up his shorts. Elastic snapped around his waist. Then the sweatpants. He fumbled, trying to tie the cord with numb fingers.

Dead.

She was dead.

When he wiped the sweat from his face with his sleeve, blood oozed from the bite on his hand. It sickened him. He gagged and retched again.

He staggered to his feet. He was weak and lightheaded and empty. The fever that had consumed him for so long had burned out in one violent explosion.

It was as if he'd always been two people. One was lonely, wanting love, wanting to be close to someone. The other self raged at her fear of him and struck out at her refusal. That violent self had—he choked on the word—lusted.

And killed.

His lonely self cowered, sick now with remorse and fear.

He braced himself against a charred upright. Cold rain seeping through what was left of the roof shocked him back to his senses.

He had to shake off this terror. He had to think.

He listened, gasping, then held his breath. No sound but the pounding of his blood. The patter of rain and the whistle of wind. The rumble of cars on the sunken roadway.

He edged his way cautiously to the open doorway. He peered out.

No one.

Only the stroller.

The red plastic truck had fallen to the sidewalk. The little boy's eyes were wide open now.

They stared straight at him.

THREE

WALT EDWIN'S SPIKES clattered on the sidewalk. He yelled over his shoulder. "Hey, man, I gotta piss! Here's the men's room!"

Jim Kent guffawed. It was a standing joke. They always stopped here to relieve themselves after the ball game. Then they'd go over to Amsterdam and have a beer. Tough shit they'd had to quit when they were down four to three in the fifth.

Jim's mouth dropped open. "What the fuck!"

A white kid. Maybe about two years old. He was sitting in a stroller, his little face screwed up and wet with tears and raindrops. Even as Jim looked, he stood up and put one small, determined leg over the side of the stroller. Jim looked around. no parent. No baby-sitter. Looked like someone had just run off and left him.

Jim knelt down beside the boy, who, out of the stroller now, was clutching a grubby piece of blanket and wailing. "Whatsa matter, little dude?" asked Jim. "Where's your mama?"

Walt was back. Too quickly. Jim looked up. Walt's face was ashy and his mouth was working strangely.

"Man, what the shit's the matter with you?"

Walt's answer was to double over and vomit. When his convulsion passed, he wiped his mouth with the back of his hand. "Oh, shit, man! Oh Jesus! We gotta get out of here!"

"What you tellin' me?"

"Go look if you gotta. Be quick."

In seconds Jim was back, sick and shuddering. They consulted in frightened whispers. Lingering was fatal. If anyone saw them here, they were as good as convicted and sentenced.

But what should they do about this kid standing there with his little mouth square with anguish? The dead lady must be his mama. They should take him to a police station. They should report they'd found a body.

They knew what would happen if they turned up at the police station with a white kid whose mama lay raped and dead in the ruins behind them.

The child's sobs were louder now. His wails were turning to screams. Any minute someone might come by.

Walt looked around. They were lucky so far. No one to hear the child yelling, no one to know he and Jim had been anywhere near this place. No one but the kid who was toddling away from them now, dragging his blanket through the leaves and puddles on the sidewalk. He had left the stroller and the toy truck behind him.

Suddenly the hairs stood up on the back of Walt's neck. "Oh shit, man," he cried in a hoarse, desperate whisper. "Run!"

They had splashed all the way out of the park, dodged the cars on Central Park West, and were well into the huge apartment complex that filled the blocks to Amsterdam before Walt stopped running. He looked fearfully behind him.

"What the fuck's the matter with you?" Jim panted. He wiped the rain from his face.

"Didn't you see him?"

"See who?"

"The man."

"You shittin' me? I didn't see no man."

"In the bushes. Back there." Walt glanced over his shoulder again.

"White man?"

"Dunno. Only saw his legs. He was wearin' blue sweats."

Jim's face was gray now. His voice was a whisper. "Think he's the one who—?"

"Dunno. But that sucker seen us."

In the deepening twilight with rain splashing steadily down on them, Walt and Jim looked at each other. Their eyes were white with fear.

FOUR

"GET THE FACTS. Check out the site. Interview the family."

Those were orders.

"Yes, sir," said Michael Marlowe to the metropolitan editor. The assignment he dreaded had come, as he'd known it must ever since he got his job as reporter for the *Courier*.

Half an hour later Mike was clenching his jaw and trying to keep his face from showing what he felt. He was a reporter. Reporters, like this cop who was giving the facts about the crime, should not get emotional over the stories they were sent to cover, no matter what particular horror it might have for them personally. None of the other media people here in the Central Park police station seemed to be moved.

Detective Hector García, a small slender man with the face of a grieving monkey, was heading the investigation.

The victim, twenty-two-year-old Lorna Meyers, a Caucasian female, had been identified by her uncle, Henry Meyers. Her home was with her sister in Kew Gardens. She was a graduate student at Columbia.

She had been raped, then strangled.

The case had a bizarre and terrible twist. Lorna Meyers was also a baby sitter. She had taken two-year-old Ricky Foster, only child of Pat and Rowland Foster of West 92nd Street, to play in the park, their usual activity on these mild October afternoons. A woman had just called the police to tell them that she had seen and talked with Lorna and Ricky earlier in the day. Jeanette Ruiz, of West 100th Street, told the police that Ricky played almost every day with her little girl, Robin. Lorna and Ricky had left the playground about three o'clock to meet someone on the east side of the park. Jeanette Ruiz did not know anything about the person they were going to meet.

Rain coming down hard about five o'clock had sent everyone hurrying from the park.

Lorna did not make it back to West 92nd Street.

Neither did Ricky Foster.

The scene of her death was a burned-out comfort station in a secluded spot not far from the 96th Street exit on the west side of Central Park. Although the abandoned structure was screened by trees and bushes, the area around it was usually heavily populated on a warm afternoon—joggers, skaters, ballplayers, children, older people sitting in the sun.

The sudden rainfall had emptied the area. If Lorna Meyers had screamed, no one, not even the players on the field just the other side of the hedge, had heard her.

She'd been found by four members of one ball team, whose habit was to stop after their game to use the comfort station for its original purpose. They had run to the nearest police station, the 24th precinct on 100th Street near Amsterdam, and blurted out their ghastly find. Police arriving at the scene a few minutes later found an abandoned stroller on the sidewalk a few yards away from the ruin where the girl lay.

Pat Foster had identified the stroller and a red plastic toy truck found on the sidewalk beside the stroller.

Ricky had disappeared. So had the blanket he dragged with him wherever he went.

Several voices asked at once, "How about those ballplayers?"

"We have no reason to think that they—or any one of them—raped and killed Lorna Meyers. It was not a gang rape. They were afraid, but they did report. Many in their situation would have run, afraid to be involved or suspected."

"Did they see the little boy?"

"They said they did not. They were in a hurry and they didn't stop to look around. Two of them say they think they remember the stroller and the truck."

"Can you fix the time of death?"

"She hadn't been dead very long when the body was found at five-thirty, but we'll know better when we get the full report from the medical examiner."

"Do you think the child's been kidnapped?"

"The Fosters have received no ransom demands."

"What are you doing to recover the child?"

"We've got men searching the park. Darkness and rain aren't helping their efforts. Tomorrow we'll drag the lakes and the reservoir. We've started and will continue a building-by-building search of empty buildings and lots near the park and questioning of residents. When the weather clears, hopefully tomorrow, we'll talk to people in the park and find someone who saw the girl and the child. Or saw a man with them."

"Do you think Ricky will be found alive?"

García's answer was as blunt as the question. "He knows who killed Lorna Meyers."

"A two-year-old? Can a kid that age make an identification?"

"If you'd just raped and murdered, would you stop to analyze what a two-year-old could do?"

"Jesus!" There were other exclamations now, less reverent. The professional calm of these seasoned reporters was finally shattered. Mike could hardly hold down his revulsion. Tragic enough that another young woman was the victim of a brutal rape. Now an innocent child was at risk, quite likely in the hands of a psychopath.

He wrote down the names García gave out. Jeanette Ruiz and her little girl, Robin. The ballplayers who had found the body. The dead girl's next of kin, her sister Linda.

"No parents?" he asked the detective.

"Both dead. The sister is four years older than the victim."

"How did Jeanette Ruiz know the victim was Lorna Meyers?"

"She was listening to the radio while she was fixing supper. Heard the first report of a body and a missing child. She recognized Lorna and Ricky from the description."

"Anyone else come up with information?"

"Not yet." García stood up. The interview was over. "Ladies and gentlemen, that's all we have right now. We hope you'll work with us closely on this one. This kind of crime needs as much publicity as it can get. We want people who saw the girl to come forward. The Fosters may go on TV with a plea to the kidnapper."

"How are they taking it?"

"Shocked, unbelieving. Hoping he's just lost and wandering around in the park. Or that he fell asleep someplace. That may be true. If so we'll find him when daylight comes."

Mike caught the detective's eyes. Would Ricky Foster still be alive when daylight came? He could see the answer in García's melancholy face. The chances were very slight that a two-year-old would survive a night's exposure to the autumn rain and cold.

"Are the Fosters talking to the media?" he asked.

"Not yet. They're upset by the lights and equipment all over the street in front of their building. I know that's how you people do your jobs, but I hope after you get your stories for the eleven o'clock news, you'll let the Fosters get some rest."

Mike thanked the detective. When the others began to straggle out, he hung behind to ask García the exact location of the murder site.

He was deeply depressed when he left the police station. He pulled the collar of his trench coat up against the rain and rapidly walked west.

He knew he had to get a grip on himself. He had to come to terms with this assignment. He was twenty-eight and still on probation at the *Courier*. If he handled this story well, his future was decided.

He'd come from Denver three years ago to go to the Columbia Graduate School of Journalism. After a couple of years on a suburban daily, he'd gotten this job. His break had come when he covered the breaking of a drug ring that had operated in the local junior and senior high school. Those stories had netted him a Page One Award and the clips that had impressed the editors at the *Courier*. He was still awed when he saw his byline.

Selling drugs to children was one thing, bad enough, but rape was another. This crime went far beyond what he'd learned to stomach of the routine violence of the city. Personal feelings could cloud his thinking and distort his judgement.

He could still hear Julie weeping as if she would never stop, and see his mother and father growing old before his eyes.

On Central Park West he caught an uptown bus. At 92nd Street, police barricades and floodlights showed where the news people were gathered in front of the Fosters' brownstone.

The editor had split the story—given the Fosters to Ed Sheely and the Meyers family to Mike. Mike didn't know which assignment was tougher—to try to talk to parents whose only child was missing, or to a young woman whose sister had been raped and murdered.

Reporters and camera crews had badgered his family until they felt as if they were under siege. He'd hoped that if his intended career in journalism ever brought him into contact with a rape victim or her family, he could get his story without bringing pressure that only exacerbated their pain. Now he was put to the test.

Above 96th Street the neighborhood changed. Buildings were less cared for, the street was dirtier. The line that 96th Street drew across Manhattan was a barrier separating affluence from poverty, white from black, except in the enclave around Columbia University.

He got off the bus and hurried into the park where he saw the pale glow of lights. Rain gusted, and moving shadows swayed and whispered. Lights flickered like fireflies where police with powerful flashlights searched for Ricky Foster. The branches overhead swayed and dipped, and leaves hit the sidewalk with a flurry of soft, wet noises.

The rain had kept all but the stoutest curiosity-seekers away. Mike saw furtive glances and heard mumbled speculation about his identity when he showed his press pass to the cop on guard at the roped-off site.

He was permitted to look at the ugly spot where Lorna Meyers had met death. The outline of the body was marked on the crumbling tile floor. Papers, garbage, bottles, beer cans, used condoms, and the stench of stale urine showed the uses this derelict structure had been put to.

The ground around it was trampled and muddy. "Any footprints?" he asked the cop.

"Whoever was here got mud on his shoes, but all the pairs of feet in spikes pretty much obliterated any prints. Rain's washing everything away. By daylight we'll get a better look at what's left.''

Mike jotted a few notes. There was nothing more he could learn here. Now he had to go to Queens to talk to the dead girl's family. He almost hoped that Linda Meyers, like the Fosters, would refuse to speak to the media tonight. If he had to face her and ask questions, he knew he would be violating her privacy and forcing her to expose her deepest feelings.

It took him more than an hour to reach the two-story building where Lorna had lived with her sister. This, too, was being guarded by cops and assaulted by men and women with TV cameras and lights and microphones. His depression was compounded now with a deep disgust. For all his sensitivity to this issue, he was no better than the crowd that stood behind the police lines and elbowed and jostled and murmured. The rain had ceased. The gawkers and the ghouls had come out.

He recognized a reporter from *Newsday*. They'd met covering a fatal fire in Long Island City a few months ago. Mike pushed his way into the circle of news people. "Jerry," he said, "what's happening?"

"Hi, Mike. Not a fucking thing. The sister is in there with her aunt and uncle. An old man in a backwards collar paid a call, stayed half an hour. Came out and preached a sermon about invasion of privacy."

"Anything from the family?"

"Not a word. Neighbors say the same crap we hear at every tragedy. The Meyers girls were quiet and minded their own business. Came here from Brooklyn nine years ago. Only one item which may or may not be relevant—lady upstairs says Lorna Meyers was good-looking. The sister, too, she says."

The door of the building opened. A wave went through the crowd. The murmurs grew louder. Lights went up, bathing the scene in a white glow. Cameras began to click and whirr. As the crowd of reporters closed in, Mike was pushed almost to the front steps. The cop at the door stepped aside. A slight, gray-haired man came through the door.

"That's the uncle!" Jerry hissed.

Voices erupted. "Look this way, Mr. Meyers!" "Mr. Meyers, will you tell us—"

Henry Meyers stood on the top step. He looked out over the noisy mob, blinking in the glare. The door behind him was still open. Another person slipped through it and came out to stand beside him.

Linda Meyers. Mike had never seen her, but he knew. For a second the crowd hushed. Mike looked at the slim, dark-haired woman whose face was white and rigid. He wanted to reach out to her, tell her to go back inside. He wanted to shelter her from what he knew was coming,

Lights flashed. The voices exploded this time.

"Miss Meyers, look this way!"

"How did you feel when you heard your sister had been raped?"

"Did she have any boyfriends?"

"What would you like to see happen to the man who did it?"

Henry Meyers lifted his hand. The clamor died. "My niece, Linda, has asked me to make this statement on behalf of the family of Lorna Meyers. We hope that after you've heard it, you will go away and leave us to our grief."

"Hurry up or you won't make the eleven o'clock news," a voice behind Mike called out.

Henry Meyers seemed not to have heard. He drew a piece of paper from his breast pocket and began to read. "We have lost Lorna in a vicious crime. We know of no one who would have wished her harm. She was a lovely girl, a good girl—" His voice faltered. Tears glittered on his pale cheeks. Beside him Linda Meyers closed her eyes. She swayed slightly. For a moment Mike thought she was going to faint. Then she opened her eyes and stared blindly over the crowd.

Henry Meyers had recovered. He went on, "We deeply sympathize with Mr. and Mrs. Foster, whose little boy is missing. We urge anyone who saw Lorna today to contact the police. Tell them where and when you saw her. If you help the police identify the killer, you may help return Ricky to his parents. That is all we have to say at this time. We beg you now to leave us alone."

He stepped back. The attack began again. "When's the funeral?" one voice cried. Henry Meyers turned his back.

Linda went inside. Her uncle was behind her. The policeman closed the door.

"That's all, folks!" said Jerry. "See you at the funeral, Mike, whenever it is!"

The camera crews began to collect their gear. The neighbors were dispersing now. They'd go home and turn on TV, hoping to catch a glimpse of themselves when the tapes were aired.

Mike stayed where he was for a few minutes, writing down what he could remember of Henry Meyers' statement. Then he looked around. The rain had stopped. Misty haloes wreathed the lights on the tree-lined street, which was becoming quiet as the crowd thinned.

Reporters were still bunched around a woman standing in front of the building. Mike edged close enough to hear her identify herself as Adelaide Huffman. She lived in the apartment above Linda. She, apparently, had been the source of information about the beauty of the Meyers sisters. She had not been wrong about Linda.

To Mike's question about the minister who had visited earlier, she replied, "No, he isn't a local man. He's from St. Paul's in Brooklyn where the girls used to live. His name is Reinhardt Schmidt." She turned away from Mike and answered another reporter's question—"How did I feel? I felt sick, just sick, when I heard. Lorna was such a sweet girl, so pretty and so quiet. It just goes to show you—"

Mike wrote down the name of the minister. He'd try to talk with him. First he had to get an interview with Linda Meyers. His editor would not be satisfied with the uncle's statement.

He waited until the rest of the media people had left. Only a few of the curious spectators remained. And the cop in front of the door.

No assignment in his entire career would ever be as hard as this one. He was about to pull a trick a reporter had pulled on his family. He'd hated the man who had done it, and he hated himself now.

But once inside her apartment, he would keep his promise to treat the rape victim's family with dignity and respect.

On a clean page of his notebook he wrote quickly. "Miss Meyers: Rape stories invite the worst kind of speculation about the victim. You may read upsetting things about your sister in tomorrow's paper. My name is Michael Marlowe. I'm a reporter with the *Courier*. If you'll give me a brief interview, I'll make sure that only the straight facts appear in my story."

He tore the page from his book, folded it, and wrote her name on the outside. Then he went up the front steps and held the note out to the cop. "Would you please give this to Miss Meyers?"

"If you're from the media, you're wasting your time."

"Just give it to her, that's all I ask. It's something she'll want to know."

The cop was young. Guard duty was boring. But he was not stupid. He opened the note and read it. "Show me your ID," he said.

Mike held out his press pass. The policeman looked at it. "OK. I'll give this to Miss Meyers. But don't expect anything."

He went inside. In a few minutes he was back. Mike didn't know which of them was the more surprised when the cop told him he could go in.

FIVE

"MOMMY! Mommy!"

His throat hurt. His nose was stuffed up. His diaper was full and wet and smelly.

His eyelids seemed stuck together. He dragged them open. All he could see was dark. Then a flicker of light. It moved, closer and closer, so bright now that he had to squeeze his eyes shut again.

Where was Mommy? Where was Worna?

"What's the matter, little Billie boy? What's the matter with my baby?" The voice was old and quivery, like Mister Boo's voice. But this voice wasn't nice. It was scary.

He put his thumb in his mouth and clutched his blanket. It smelled bad, like the hard, bare mattress he was lying on. He began to cry.

He was cold. He wanted Worna to give him his warm bath and put on clean diapers and his pajamas. He was hungry. His tummy hurt. He wanted Mommy to give him his supper and then hold him and rock him until he fell asleep.

When he woke up, he'd be in his own bed with his blanket and his teddy bear.

Arms picked him up. They were skinny and hard. They held him tight against a rough, bad-smelling old coat. He stiffened and began to struggle.

"Don't do that, Billie!" The old voice was sharp now. "Be good!"

The arms put him down again. The mattress sagged as someone sat down beside him. Beneath him the springs made funny, pinging noises.

Hard, scratchy hands wrapped his blanket around him. Then the arms picked him up again and held him. Someone was rocking him back and forth.

It wasn't Mommy. It wasn't Worna. It was someone who was squeezing him so tight he could hardly breathe. He had to make this bad person let go of him. He began to kick.

"Stop that, you little shit!" The voice was rough and angry. The arms loosened their hold. He kicked harder. Then a hand smacked him across the face. When he opened his mouth to scream, the hand hit him harder, again and again.

Finally he lay quiet, sobbing softly and trying to choke down the blood that filled his mouth.

"That's my own darling Billie. You're good and quiet now," the old voice crooned in his ear. He let the arms pick him up again and made no struggle as he was rocked back and forth. Blood trickled out of his mouth. He closed his eyes and sobbed and slipped into the dark.

"That's my good little boy. Sleep, my baby Billie. I'll take care of you. I'll never let them take you away from me again!"

SIX

"SIT DOWN, Mr. Marlowe." Linda Meyers spoke with a weariness that seemed beyond all caring. She barely glanced at the press pass Mike held out. Her shoulder drooped, and her slender body seemed fragile in a dark suit and sweater.

He was moved to such pity that, for a moment, he debated. He could tell her that he understood what she was going through in a way that others, no matter how close and how sympathetic, never could. He had seen a person he loved utterly destroyed. His family had been shattered.

No, he wouldn't tell her about his own tragedy. She would think he was trying to buy her confidence. Besides, there was a rock-hard truth. He could only imagine, never really know, what rape meant to a woman.

He dropped his trench coat on a chair inside the door and followed Linda into the living room. White walls, low couches, floor-to-ceiling bookshelves. It was a tract apartment with boxlike spaces, but its simplicity appealed to him.

Henry Meyers came in from the kitchen just as Mike sat down. He stood up.

"This is Michael Marlowe, Uncle Henry, from the *Courier*."

Henry Meyers did not offer to shake hands. He glared at Mike. "I think Linda's making a big mistake, letting you in here, but I'm not going to argue with her. Just don't you upset her! She's had about as much today as one human being can stand."

"I'll try not to, sir," Mike said.

Linda had seated herself stiffly on one of the couches. She looked like a person braced for punishment for something she hadn't done.

When Henry Meyers left the room, Mike took a corner seat that faced her. "Miss Meyers, the first thing I want you to know is that I'm truly sorry. And I'm grateful that you agreed to talk to me. I hope it will be worth the effort you're willing to make."

She nodded. "I hope so, too." Her next words surprised and touched him, "Would you like a cup of coffee, Mr. Marlowe?"

When he looked into her eyes he understood. The offer of coffee was a stall. She was dreading this interview as much as she had hated the blinding lights and shouted questions outside. He wanted to agree with Uncle Henry that this was a big mistake, grab his coat, and run.

But he couldn't. He was a reporter and he'd gotten this far. He'd gained a little of her trust. And if he handled this right, he might, in some small way, make up for the brutal treatment she'd gotten so far from the media.

"No thank you, no coffee," he said. "I'll try not to take too much of your time." He wouldn't use his notebook. "Miss Meyers," he began, "I'm sure you know that a surprisingly high percentage of rapes are committed by men who are not strangers to the women they attack. People will ask if the man could have been someone she knew, someone she was meeting in the park."

Linda shook her head. "Impossible. Lorna wasn't like that."

"Like what?"

"She wasn't a woman who attracted men."

"She didn't have any boyfriends?"

"Lorna didn't date. I worry—worried—that she had no social life. She didn't dress in a way that invited attention. She was wearing a blue-jean skirt and a cotton shirt with a corduroy jacket when she went out to go to her class . . . this morning." He knew that hesitation meant bewildered disbelief. "Only this morning—"

"What did she tell you about her job?"

"She said Ricky was a good little boy, affectionate and easy to care for. Lorna loved him. If anyone had threatened him, she would have tried to save him. That's why I'm sure she was"— Linda set her jaw and took a deep breath—"before Ricky was kidnapped."

"Did she ever say anything about people she and Ricky saw in the park? I don't mean the rapist. I mean anybody."

"No. The police asked me that, too. Lorna didn't talk much about herself or what she did. She was very quiet, reticent. She and I had an unspoken agreement that we would not pry into each other's lives. I'll regret for the rest of my life that I didn't know more—that we weren't closer."

Mike made a small gesture. "How could you know...?" he said, then stopped, realizing how inadequate he sounded. Her eyes met his for a few seconds. Then he asked, "What was she studying at Columbia?"

"Psychology. She was always curious about human behavior."

"Career goals?"

"She hoped to be a child psychologist. She liked children."

This was not material from which good copy was made. Mike could almost hear his editor's contempt—"What is this kid-glove interview, Marlowe? Are you a reporter or a fucking psychiatrist?"

The editor wanted the shocked, emotional response to the kind of questions that had been shouted out in front of the building. Mike needed to know her feelings to write a good story, but he could not bring himself to ask about them.

"What are you going to put in your story, Mr. Marlowe?" she asked. He almost jumped.

"I'll start by describing the place where it happened. I went there after the police briefing tonight."

"Tell me about it. The police didn't."

As carefully as he could, sparing her the uglier details of the place of Lorna's defilement and death, he described the comfort station and its isolation in the midst of the park. Her dark eyes were fastened on his the whole time. They were dry. She still seemed to be shocked beyond tears.

"Is there anything you particularly want me to say in my story? About Lorna? About how you feel about the man who did it?"

"I've told you everything about Lorna that could possibly be relevant. You won't speculate? Sensationalize?"

"No, you can count on me not to do that."

"That's why I agreed to talk to you. I want Lorna's image to be as unclouded as she was, in spite of this terrible thing."

Her trust moved him. "I'll do my best to keep it that way."

"As for me, I can't tell you my feelings. I can hardly even *feel* them yet. I know men take out their hatred of women this way, but I still can't believe a man did that to Lorna and then... killed..." Her voice thinned.

He could tell her that sometimes they don't kill, but leave the victim so maimed in body and mind that she might as well be dead. Something dies inside.

He stood up. The information she had given him, along with what he could get from the minister, would have to be enough. At the door he shrugged quickly into his coat. "Thank you, Miss Meyers, and goodbye." He held out his hand. After a second's hesitation, she took it. Her small cold fingers were closed in his for a brief moment.

"Good night, Mister Marlowe." The door closed behind him and the chain rattled into the bolt.

Mike walked along the quiet streets where puddles were rippled by a strong wind that was blowing the storm out to sea. Tomorrow would be fair. The police would be in Central Park to question the people who came out into the sun.

His depression returned, and with it a sharp realization. He was lonely. The family tragedy he had left behind him when he came to New York had been a restraining shadow. He had allowed no one to get close to him.

He'd been home a few times. His father was gray with silent pain, and his mother had developed a habit of quickly putting her hand over her mouth to hide her trembling lips. Julie was calmer, but that was all.

Work had been his anodyne. Now it was wearing off. Lorna Meyers' death had unlocked his buried feelings. For the first time he'd met a woman he knew he could talk to, one who would understand the shadow over him, one who would not close off his admissions of rage and helplessness.

But the time and place could not be more wrong. Ironically, what brought them together was a tragedy so profound he knew she would never be able to see him as anything but a reminder of this terrible time. He would never have a chance to get to know Linda Meyers.

SEVEN

WHEN THE TAXI dropped Mike off, lights were still burning on the porch and behind the gothic windows of the narrow house separated from the brown stones of St. Paul's Lutheran Church by a strip of dark lawn. Both century-old buildings were dwarfed by the shabby apartment buildings that had crowded around them. Papers and plastic food containers littered the sidewalk in front of the church where a sign futilely begged, No Loitering, Please.

Mike rang the doorbell of the parsonage and heard its distant peal. Through the oval glass panel of the front door he saw a dimly lighted hall. Then a tall figure, dark and indistinct, appeared. "Who is it?" a voice asked cautiously.

"I'm Michael Marlowe from the *Courier*, Reverend Schmidt. I'd like to ask you some questions about Lorna Meyers."

"It's very late."

"I know, sir, but it's important. I have to get a story and I know you're a reliable source."

The man who opened the door was slightly stooped, with thinning gray hair and tired eyes. Tight lines in his face and a compressed, downturned mouth suggested to Mike that Reinhardt Schmidt might have spent too many years trying to minister in a deteriorating parish.

He was affable, however, as he led the way to the back of the house. "A shocking tragedy, Mr. Marlowe. I don't know what I can tell you about Lorna, but I'll try to answer your questions."

Mike looked around the high-ceilinged study. A cluttered desk, somber ranks of religious books in a glass-fronted case. A stale smell of age, dust and sanctity. The minister sank into a leather chair behind the desk. He tapped on its arms with long, nervous fingers. Then he sighed. "When will women learn?" he asked.

"Learn what, sir?" asked Mike, surprised.

"When will women realize they cannot run around alone in the parks of this city?"

Mike sat down in the chair Schmidt had motioned him to. "Lorna Meyers was only doing what hundreds of other women were doing in the city today—taking a child out to play," he said.

"An unnecessary risk, in my opinion. Lorna may not have outgrown a certain childish lack of prudence."

Mike edged forward. He had to guard against showing an unprofessional eagerness. Nothing in Linda's description of her sister had prepared him to hear Lorna described as imprudent. "You've known the Meyers family for some time?" he asked the minister.

"I baptized both girls. Buried both parents."

"How long ago was that?"

"Nine years. Lorna was thirteen, Linda in her last year of high school. After she graduated, she sold the house, and the girls moved away. I thought they should have stayed in this parish where people knew them and loved them, but Linda was determined to make a new life for herself and her sister."

"How did their parents die? Accident?"

"No. Harold had cancer. It took a year. Ruth was so exhausted that she had no strength to battle pneumonia that followed flu. She died three months after Harold."

"How did Linda and Lorna take their loss? They were very young."

"Linda's faith was sorely tried. This blow today has brought her very near despair. It will be a long time before she is able to forgive."

"To forgive the killer? Surely that's asking too much!"

"Linda's bitterness will lessen when she's had time to reflect. And to pray. If we call upon him, the Lord never lets us be tempted beyond our strength." The last words came with such an automatic piety that Mike was sure the Reverend Schmidt had long ago ceased to think about their meaning.

"I admire Linda," the minister went on. "She became the head of the family when her parents died. She went to work after high school, but she managed to get her B.A. by taking courses at night. Lorna pursued a similar course and had entered upon graduate studies. She, too, is to be commended. But Lorna—"

"What about Lorna?"

Schmidt smiled, a thin smile that brought no amusement to his face. His tapered fingers, touching now, made a steeple of his hands. "Linda, when I knew them years ago, was always quiet and studious. Lorna was quite different. What you might call an extrovert. She grew up very fast."

"After her parents died, you mean?"

"Then . . . yes. But I was referring to an earlier time. Lorna matured early."

"Matured?"

"Developed. Physically." Schmidt looked down at his steepled fingers. "When I ponder the meaning of her terrible death, I can but wonder at the mysterious ways in which the Lord moves—"

"What you're suggesting is that Lorna Meyers asked for what she got?" Mike checked himself. He had raised his voice.

"No one asks for violent death." Schmidt's mouth was a prim line now.

Mike could almost hear the unspoken "but" hovering in the room. He was having a hard time controlling himself. "You do think she asked to be raped!"

"Who's to judge what rape is, Mr. Marlowe? What's the line a man crosses between a normal male response and the loss of restraint? The man who did this is a pitiable creature, as deeply in need of the Lord's mercy as you and I."

"This 'pitiable creature' you describe, sir, violated and strangled a young woman! Kidnapped and probably killed an innocent child!"

Schmidt bowed his head and folded his hands. "I will pray for the Fosters' little boy. And for Linda's peace. Some good will come of this tragedy, Mr. Marlowe. Young women will be reminded that they cannot go about alone without incurring great risk."

Mike had to protest. "Central Park was full of people today! So was Prospect Park—old people sitting on benches, parents with their children, kids playing and riding bikes. Until the rain started, the park was as safe for Lorna and Ricky as your church!''

Schmidt sighed heavily, a sigh that had the sound of defeat. ''St. Paul's used to be a place where the young people of this parish found wholesome outlets for their energy. They studied the Bible, went bowling, sang hymns and folk songs, entertained one another with their talents like music, magic tricks, puppetry—''

Mike welcomed Schmidt's lapse into nostalgia. The minister, lost in his own thoughts, was oblivious to the anger Mike feared was showing in his face. Besides, Schmidt's reference to the past gave him a chance to steer the conversation back to Lorna Meyers.

''Did you have many young people in the church?''

''At one time—some years ago, of course—our youth group, the Luther League as we called it, numbered more than sixty.''

Mike knew it would not be tactful to ask how many came to the Luther League now. He would bet that folksinging and Bible study no longer kept parish youth uncontaminated by the lustier pleasures of secular Brooklyn.

''It's all changed now,'' said Schmidt, almost as if he'd heard Mike's inner commentary. ''So few of the old families left in the neighborhood. The newer elements just aren't interested in church. The young people are so crude, so hostile. Back in the old days our youngsters were so well brought up that I rarely had to admonish them. The few who got boisterous always apologized after I counseled them.''

''Lorna and Linda were members of your Luther League?''

''Only Lorna. Until her father became ill, that is.''

''Let me ask you this. You said that you regret that Linda lost her faith, as you put it. How about Lorna? Did her faith sustain her throughout the ordeal of those deaths?''

''At the time of Lorna's confirmation, when she was twelve, I was sure that her confession of faith was genuine. Of her state of mind at her death, I have no idea. I've seen almost nothing of the Meyers girls since they moved. When I heard of the tragedy, I went at once to Linda to offer my help. I'm grateful that she wants me to take the funeral. Arrangements aren't complete, but it will take place on Thursday afternoon.''

"Here?"

"No. When Linda saw what happened outside her building tonight, she feared that the size of St. Paul's would attract a horde of publicity-seekers. She wants a private service—only family and close friends—at a funeral home. I hope you media people will not make a circus out of it by bringing all that equipment!"

Mike held up his notebook. "This is all I'll bring."

"The media must stop hounding Linda Meyers."

"We agree on that, sir. However, covering the story is my job, just as the funeral is yours. The more publicity, the better the chance of identifying the killer and finding Ricky Foster."

"I will pray that it be so."

On the series of subways he had to take to get back to the city room, Mike scribbled notes from both interviews, notes that he would later enter into his computer file on Lorna Meyers. Then he tried to think through a coherent lead for his story.

Impossible.

The two descriptions of Lorna simply did not match. Schmidt, whom Mike could not think of without the words "sanctimonious" and "hypocrite," may not have known just what his words implied, but he had described a girl with a lively personality and a precocious sexual maturity. Dynamite, surely, in a church youth group. He wondered if Schmidt had ever been compelled to "counsel" Lorna.

To her sister, Lorna had been shy, reserved, and not attractive to men. Linda did not want that image to be "clouded."

In the hands of another reporter, Schmidt's version of Lorna could be slanted into just the kind of story Linda did not want. In spite of the publicity that had forced improvement in the handling of rape stories, there were always believers in the myths about sex crimes. Even in Julie's case, questions had been asked: "Who does she run around with?" "Does she take drugs?" "What kind of girl is she, anyway?"

Just as the train pulled into 42nd Street, Mike saw another possibility. Linda had sadly admitted that she and her sister did not know much about each other's private lives. Perhaps Linda did not know that "other Lorna," that outgoing girl whose warmth might have seemed—to someone—like an invitation.

EIGHT

WHEN THE DOOR CLOSED behind Michael Marlowe, Reinhardt Schmidt found himself trembling. He was exhausted.

Had he said too much? Or too little?

What did Michael Marlowe, a product of this permissive culture, know of sin?

Clearly the young reporter thought that Lorna was the victim of a man's uncontrolled lust. He didn't understand that fornication is a sin, committed by two who have fallen from grace.

His Prussian father, stern and ascetic, and a minister like himself, had warned him of the danger of the sins of the flesh. He still could feel the pain of the switch on his bare legs and buttocks and the deeper pain of his shame after his father caught him in the bathroom abusing himself with the magazine open to the pictures of women—naked—their breasts and . . . those other parts . . .

Schmidt had to wipe his forehead suddenly dewed with sweat. He'd learned the lesson. Women's bodies were the source of defilement of men. He'd never let himself even consider marriage, knowing that once he allowed himself to enjoy a woman, even in a relationship sanctioned by the church for procreation, he would become weak and neglect his duty to the Lord.

If the mere picture of a woman's body could sink him to such a depth, how much more would a real woman's naked flesh . . . ? He could still remember, in times of great weakness, the dark, shamed pleasure.

He had counseled the youth of the parish, knowing even then that they laughed behind his back at his old-fashioned ways. He had urged the girls to modesty in dress and deportment, and the boys to keeping themselves pure. "Save yourself for marriage, my boy, when the Lord will bless your physical union."

He did not say those things now. Young people today would laugh, not behind his back, but in his face. The battle he fought was over almost before he had begun. In his twenty-five years in the parish of St. Paul's, he had seen the end of everything he valued—patriotism, reverence for God and his church, cleanliness and decency.

The worst of it was the descent of morality into the hell of public lust and filth and perversion. Women painted their faces and bared their nakedness to entertain men. They drew them toward vile thoughts and viler deeds.

He turned out the porch light and made sure the door was bolted. Back in his study, he sat down again behind his desk and opened his worn Bible to a passage in the Book of Proverbs that he had been wont to use when he counseled the young men back in the days when they had listened to him:

For the commandment is a lamp and the teaching a light
    and the reproofs of discipline are a way of life,
To preserve you from the evil woman, from the smooth
    tongue of the adventuress.
Do not desire her beauty in your heart
    and do not let her capture you with her eyelashes.

Lorna Meyers' eyelashes had been long and curling, and where they lay against her cheek, they sparkled with tears.

NINE

HAROLD BLOOR rolled his wheelchair from the kitchen to the front room of his tiny apartment. Yesterday when he'd waved goodbye to Ricky and Lorna, he'd feared he would not see them again. If the rain had continued through today, they would not come to the park.

But the sun shone high and golden in a deep blue sky. He was humming when he put on his jacket and rolled himself out the door and down the ramp to the street. He'd buy a paper and read it while he waited for them. He didn't watch TV. Too noisy. Too hard on his eyes. He liked to get his news from the paper.

Lorna was such a fine young woman, gentle and modest. Not like most of them these days. He saw too many rude ones, loud and vulgar ones, who swooped down on him on their roller skates or marched four abreast across the sidewalk and dared him to run them down with his chair.

Ricky and Lorna had come into his life such a short time ago, but already the hours he spent with them these autumn afternoons were the high point of his life. After months of loneliness since Harriet died, he had someone to talk to. Someone who listened. He had something to look forward to.

Someone who loved him.

Ricky! The little boy hugged him, put his little arms around his neck and called him "Mister Boo." How the little fellow loved to be taken for a ride sitting in his lap in the electric wheelchair!

Today he'd give Ricky a long ride.

The front page of the paper had a big face on it and a bold, one-word headline. He wouldn't even try to read it until he was settled and could put on his reading glasses.

He tucked the paper down beside him in the chair and continued his slow way toward the park. He let the chair down the inclined curb onto Fifth Avenue when the light turned green. He could barely make it across on one light. He had to count on the drivers to be patient. Sometimes they were not patient. They honked at him and yelled things he was glad he could not hear.

The sun was warm today, but the air was nippy. He was glad he'd put his jacket on over his sweater. Not many days left for him to go to the park. What would he do on the long winter days when it was too cold to go outside? Maybe he could persuade Lorna to bring Ricky to his apartment. He'd make tea for Lorna and have milk and cookies for Ricky.

He passed by his favorite place near the benches on the long curving walk. Today he'd go farther into the park. He might go all the way to the ballfield and meet them. That way he could give Ricky a ride all the way back.

Not too many people out yet. There would be more when the air was warmer and when school was out for the day.

There was that repellent old creature who roamed the park with a shopping cart stuffed with rags. Poor thing! He was thankful that age had left him, so far at least, in possession of all his senses, even if it had taken the use of his legs and damaged his heart.

The old woman was heading straight toward him. He had no way to avoid her.

"Outta my way!" Her eyes met Harold's in a mad glare. "You leave me alone! I know all about you—you'll try to take Billie away from me! I won't let you. So fuck off!"

He drew the chair as far over to the edge of the sidewalk as he could. When she passed him, he got a whiff of the stink of her unwashed body and filthy clothes. Through the wire sides of the cart he could see equally filthy wads of cloth, crumpled paper bags, and a piece of something that looked like a gray blanket.

When she had gone a few yards beyond him, the squeal of wheels ceased. He looked around. She was bending over the cart, rummaging in it, rearranging the bits and pieces within. She looked up and caught him staring. "Mind your own business, you old fart!" she yelled.

He moved on. He came to a sun-dappled spot at the top of a small slope. From here he'd be able to see Ricky and Lorna when they came along the walk that edged the ballfield. The grass was smooth here, and he could safely pull the chair off the sidewalk. Then he wouldn't be in anyone's way.

He was settled at last. He fumbled in his breast pocket for his reading glasses. When he had them on, he picked up the paper and looked at the front page.

TEN

THE MAN ON THE BED writhed, twisting sheets gray and rumpled and sour with the smell of his body. It had been months since he'd taken them to the Laundromat.

Rapist!

Killer!

Kidnapper!

He wasn't any of these things! Didn't they know? Couldn't they see?

He picked up the paper from the floor where he'd flung it. The reporter's name was Michael Marlowe. He'd written this crap, this pile of lies. How could Michael Marlowe, whoever the fuck he was, know how Lorna had driven him?

He wadded up the paper and hurled it away again. He wanted to howl like a dog.

Lorna, Lorna, why didn't you let me love you? You wanted it. I know you did. You wanted it that other time, too. You would've liked it if we'd been alone long enough—if we hadn't had to hide and sneak and hurry.

I needed you, Lorna. I'd been looking for you. You shouldn't have been afraid of me. Not then and not now. You shouldn't have kicked like that and bit my hand!

Sweat broke out all over him. He writhed again and whimpered. He remembered her eyes wide open and afraid when she recognized him. Her mouth opened to scream but she stopped herself. She didn't want to wake up the kid. He'd put his hand over her mouth just in case. When her teeth sank into his flesh, he'd exploded with pain and rage. He had to hit her then. His hand on the side of her face almost knocked her out. She'd only moaned after that.

Afterwards...

The terror. She'd remember everything. She knew who he was. She would tell the cops. She would tell lies about him.

They'd snoop in his Army record. No one would believe him. He'd be arrested and sent to prison. Lorna would do that to him.

He wasn't a killer. He had to save himself. He wasn't a rapist. Lorna had wanted him. So had that gook whore. She'd lied, too.

Tears came. Then hard angry sobs that made his whole body ache. Lorna, I didn't want to hurt you! I thought I was so smart and so lucky to have found you without anybody knowing.

He'd done what he'd been told to do. Stayed away from Lorna. For years. First 'Nam, then out west. He'd tried not to think about her, not to remember. But she'd come to him in his dreams. He'd been real careful about women, even when he was wanting her so bad he was crazy-like.

He was forever seeing her. A brown-haired girl with long legs and her kind of body would be walking ahead of him, and he'd start to follow her. Then she'd turn around and look like she was scared, and he'd see she wasn't Lorna, and he'd feel like shit.

Then one day it hit him. Lorna was grown up. She wasn't a scared kid anymore. She'd know, now, how to make him happy. He'd go back. He'd find her. He'd do it right this time.

So he had come back—four, five months ago. No one knew but his sister Barbara and her schmuck of a husband. He didn't want to ask questions, so he used his smarts to track her down. He wanted to surprise her. Someone else was living in the Meyers' old place. He used the phone book and checked out the addresses of all the people listed under "L. Meyers." He hung around outside buildings and watched.

Then one day he found her. She came out of that apartment in Queens. Lorna—a woman. She was still beautiful, but kinda mousy. He liked to think that she'd been saving herself for him. He knew she'd come alive and sexy when she knew he still wanted her.

He didn't want to come right up to her on the street. He had to find just the right moment. He'd been excited, thinking how it would be when he got her alone.

The Army had taught him a lot of things. He'd hated every fucking minute of it, but he'd learned. How to stalk. How to kill quickly and silently. In 'Nam it was OK to get mad, OK to let go. He'd killed a couple of Vietcong the same way he'd killed Lorna, with his bare hands around the gook bastards' necks.

From the pocket of his jeans he pulled a wrinkled, stained bandanna. He wiped his face and blew his nose. Then he looked at the filthy rag. Sweat broke out on him again. This time he smelled the stink of his own fear.

Lorna hadn't been alone.

On top of his mind's picture of her dead, staring face, another face moved in. A little face. Its eyes stared too. Big brown eyes. Eyes that saw. Eyes that would remember.

He sat up on the bed and fished for the paper again. MISSING the bold headline screamed. Ricky Foster's face looked at him. The big dark eyes stared right into his the way they had when he'd staggered out of the ruin where Lorna lay.

He reached for a cigarette from a rumpled, nearly empty pack on the stand beside the bed. Smoke burned his lungs and made him lightheaded. He hadn't had anything to eat for two days. He'd been afraid to go anywhere, afraid to risk being seen. Finally his craving to know what was going on could no longer be satisfied by the brief reports on the TV news. He'd gone out, slipped to the newsstand on the corner to fling down his thirty cents and snatch up the *Courier*. He'd got a cup of coffee at the Chock Full O'Nuts and brought it back to his hole in the crummy West Side SRO.

He couldn't hide out here forever. Lorna was dead. He had to put that behind him. He had to think about his own survival. He had to start being cool and crafty like he'd been in the Army, like he'd been all those days he'd stalked Lorna. She had no idea he was following her until he spoke to her and the kid that day by the ballfield.

No more panic. If he'd had his shit together after he killed her, he wouldn't have run. He would've gone right up to the kid and put his hands on the stroller and wheeled him away, like he was the kid's dad. He would have gotten away with it, too. No one would have thought anything about a young father wheeling his kid home from the park when it started to pour.

Later it would have been easy to get rid of Ricky Foster.

He'd hidden in the bushes and watched the two coons find Lorna. They'd run like the devil was after them. Right then he had another chance. He should've grabbed the stroller and run after the kid. He couldn't have gone far, crying like that and dragging his blanket.

That's when he'd heard the noise, an unholy screeching that made his heart stop. Lorna! She wasn't dead! She'd come to and she was screaming. He'd panicked.

Afterwards he'd realized. She couldn't be alive, not after what he'd done to her. Someone else was screaming—one of the crazies. The park was full of them and he was in no shape to meet up with one of them. Not with...that...laying there beside him.

He'd taken off and left the kid behind for someone else to find.

He laughed, a laugh that turned into a hysterical guffaw. There really was a kidnapper, and it wasn't him! It was a big, crazy joke.

He sobered. Maybe it wasn't crazy. Maybe it wasn't even a joke.

Maybe it was a setup.

No one had kidnapped Ricky Foster. The cops had found the kid wandering around by himself. They were giving out the story he'd been kidnapped, hoping Lorna's killer would come after the witness who could give him away.

Could Ricky give him away? A two-year-old?

He couldn't take chances. "Wed wabbit!" Ricky had said. He said a lot of things real clear for a little kid.

He couldn't be careless. Never again. He had to keep up with the stories in the paper, know what the cops were doing and who they thought they were looking for.

He folded the paper to the second page and averted his eyes from the reprint of Lorna's high school graduation picture. He read slowly down the column of Michael Marlowe's story:

Police are looking for a dark-haired bearded man in his twenties. The man is five eleven or six feet and weighs about 200 pounds. He was last seen wearing a blue running suit, dark glasses and a red bandanna around his head. Anyone who saw this man in Central Park with Lorna Meyers or Ricky Foster should call the police at once.

Jesus! A description! Sweat broke out on him again. Who had seen him? The two niggers—was that why they'd run? The old guy in the wheelchair? How could it have been him—the way he peered and squinted, he had to be blind as a bat.

The only other person who might have seen him following Lorna was that old bag lady with her shopping cart full of rags. He'd seen her a lot of times when he was in the park pretending to be a jogger. Surely the cops wouldn't believe anything she said. Even at a distance he'd been able to see that the old bitch was nuts.

It had to be Ricky. He was safe at home with his mommy and daddy, and he'd lisped a description to the cops. He'd told them about a man who wore a blue suit and made a wabbit for him. A man named Warry.

The suit wasn't a problem. Not anymore. He'd been pretty quick-thinking after he got over the panic. Now he'd cut this fucking bandanna up and flush it down the toilet.

He'd been a fool to tell the kid his name. He'd been so excited being that close to Lorna again that he'd been stupid. Ricky would remember Warry. It wasn't his whole name, but it was enough. Lorna hadn't known him by that name back then. He'd called himself Bob in those days, like he did now at the messenger service where he worked.

"Bobby," Lorna had called him with that teasing lilt in her voice. True, she hadn't acted like she really liked him, but he knew she did. The rest of them treated him like he was a gorilla. He knew Lorna had to pretend she felt like they did, or they would've teased her. That was it. She had to act like she didn't like him. But she really did.

Now she was dead. And he was in worse trouble than he'd been in 'Nam. Much worse.

He stood up and crossed the narrow space to the dresser. The clouded mirror showed his blanched, greasy face and reddened eyes.

He had to show some smarts. No going back. Lorna was dead. He had to look out for himself. He had to find out if Ricky Foster really was missing. That meant watching the Fosters' building. He'd go to Lorna's funeral. No one would know him. He'd listen to what people said about the man who did it.

He'd have to look as different as possible from this description. The beard would have to go. Too bad. He liked it. It made him look tough and macho, the way he really was. He'd hate to see his face in the mirror without it.

He'd get another pair of glasses—aviator-style. They'd make him look cool. He'd slick his hair down, and later when the cops weren't looking so hard for a man with thick hair, he'd get it cut.

He scowled at his face in the mirror. The upper part was still tan from the summer. His freshly shaved chin would be pale, a dead giveaway that he'd just gotten rid of a beard. There wasn't sun enough or time enough to tan it to match.

The funeral was Thursday afternoon. He had to be ready.

Then he smiled. His white teeth looked back at him from the mirror. He'd always been ashamed of his teeth. They were small, like a little kid's teeth. Like Ricky Foster's teeth grinning at him from the front page. He'd have to be careful not to smile.

He knew what to get. He'd go to the Pathmark at Broadway and 96th Street. It was so big and so crowded no one would remember what he bought. He'd get some iodine, too, for this bite on his left hand. It hurt like hell. Maybe Lorna was getting revenge by giving him blood poisoning.

He shook his head. No more of that kind of shit!

By tomorrow he'd be unrecognizable.

ELEVEN

SEX VICTIM A LOLITA? queried a headline in the *Post* the next afternoon. Sick with dismay, Mike read the story, which was based solely on innuendo and a few suggestive adjectives.

"All right, Marlowe, where did the *Post* get this?" the editor asked.

"The source must be the minister. What he said has been twisted—"

"'What he said'? So he did give you these tidbits? Or did he confide them only to the *Post*?"

"He told me that Lorna Meyers was lively and outgoing at the age of twelve and that she had matured early."

"By matured I presume he meant her sexual maturity?"

"That was the suggestion. But he didn't know what she was like at twenty-two—he hadn't seen her in nine years!"

"Dammit, Marlowe! Look at your lead on what we printed: 'A quiet, gentle girl was brutally killed today—'"

"Her sister described her that way. I didn't think Reverend Schmidt's description was relevant or newsworthy."

"Why not? It's not libelous."

"If we do what the *Post* did with Schmidt's comments, the implications will hurt Lorna's family."

There was a short silence. Then the editor said, "What job do you hold on this paper?"

Mike swallowed hard. "I'm a reporter."

"Who am I?"

"You're the metropolitan editor."

"You're damn right I'm the editor. I'm the guy who decides what's relevant and what's newsworthy. Is that clear?"

Mike could only nod. He had slept badly and he knew that his temper was under imperfect control.

"You get the facts and the quotes and you write the story. Then I decide how much gets printed. Now do you or don't you have quotes from Schmidt about the teenage Lorna Meyers?"

"I do."

"Then get back to your screen and write the story. We'll call it 'Lorna—Another Look.'"

Mike felt his face whiten. "No, sir, I can't write it."

"Why not?"

"It distorts her character."

"You mean it distorts what you've chosen to believe of her character."

"Yes, sir."

The editor was silent. Then, without something between a sigh and a grunt, he said, "Come into my office."

Inside the office, where the glass walls shut them off from being heard, though not from being seen, by the curious in the city room, the editor said, not unkindly, "This is one of the worst kinds of stories to cover. I know how hard it is, Marlowe, not to get emotionally involved."

Encouraged, Mike replied, "The girl's sister is a very fine person. She's devastated. There are no parents."

"Are those reasons to withhold information? We have to tell our readers everything we know. Otherwise we're imposing a censorship which implies that we don't trust their intelligence. We have to let them decide for themselves. Let them realize that no woman, no matter how attractive and lively, ever really asks for rape."

"I can't continue to cover this story." Now that the truth was out, he felt an enormous relief. Sadness, too. This could cost him his job.

"Any reason besides your sympathy for the girl's family?"

The question came too close. The editor may already have guessed at Mike's personal reasons. Behind his crude language and abrasive manner was an intelligent and perceptive man. Mike knew that if he told him about Julie, he would get an understanding response.

That wasn't what he wanted. It was like asking for special treatment. If he was going to be a reporter, he had to cover the assignment he was given. If he couldn't separate his personal life and his professional life, he was through.

"I request to be taken off this story."

"Refusing an assignment is a serious matter, Mike."

"I know that."

"You're one of the best of our new reporters. I have no doubt about your future."

"Thank you, I appreciate that. But I can't work on the Meyers story."

"All right—since there's been no arrest, it's not breaking news. Ed Sheely can handle it and the Fosters. Turn your file over to him. Then go up to 96th Street and Park Avenue. You're covering a rush-hour fire in the Metro North tunnel."

Bitterly, Mike realized he had to accept the fact that the *Post*'s "cloud" over Lorna's character would be reinforced when Schmidt's "tidbits" appeared in the *Courier*. The only thing he could do was make sure that what Linda read in the *Courier* did not come from him.

At his terminal he deleted from his files his notes and everything he'd written about Lorna Meyers.

He went up to 96th Street and interviewed the coughing, weeping commuters the transit police were leading out of the smoke-filled tunnel. His heart was not in the story. He knew that his questions were banal and his information scant.

When he came back, he was summoned again into the glass-walled office. "I told you to run over your files to Ed Sheely," the editor said. "Why the fuck didn't you do it?"

"I can't. I deleted them."

"Are you out of your mind, Marlowe? Refusing an assignment is bad enough, but destroying a file to keep it out of the hands of another reporter is a damned unprofessional thing to do!"

Mike knew what he wanted. It didn't make sense. It wouldn't bring Lorna Meyers back to life. It wouldn't bring Julie back to wholeness. It wouldn't help his parents. Or Linda. But it might help him.

"I need to take a leave of absence, sir."

"I have to know why."

"It's a personal matter."

"You have to state reasons."

"Then I'll write out my letter of resignation." His jaw muscles were trembling with the effort to keep calm.

"Marlowe," said the editor with a sigh of exasperation, "I don't know what this is all about, but I know it's serious. Why don't you take a few days off, think it over?"

"No."

"Then I want you to know I think you're nuts. I'm also truly sorry to lose you."

Stunned by what he had done, Mike emptied his desk drawers. Faces were lifted from VDT screens as those closest to him in the city room watched. Carole, whose desk faced his, offered him a shopping bag. "You are off your bird, Marlowe!"

"I know," said Mike. He could not explain. When he was first assigned to the story, he had known that his personal feelings could distort his judgement. This impulse was, in all likelihood, simply a manifestation of that distortion.

But it had come from deep inside him. He was compelled to try, however futilely, to work off his failure, three years ago, to be able to do anything for his family. He had left their anguish behind him, and now he found his own anger and pain still raw.

He had a paycheck coming, and several hundred dollars in the bank. His rent was paid up. He would survive until he was clear about what he wanted to do next.

What he wanted to do right now was join the hunt for the man who had raped and murdered Lorna Meyers.

TWELVE

"RITES TODAY for Slain Baby Sitter" was the headline on the story about Lorna. "Where Is This Child?" was the latest on Ricky.

Linda sipped black coffee and read quickly through the story about the funeral. In a few minutes she would have to get ready for that ordeal, which would begin the moment she came out of the door of her building and had to fight her way to the funeral home's limousine through the shouted questions and clicking cameras.

"You ought to eat something, Linda!"

"No thanks, Aunt Liz. I'm not hungry."

"I wish you hadn't decided to invite folks back here after the service. I know it's hospitable, but it's going to be so hard on you. Please have a piece of coffee cake. How about a nice ham sandwich? So many people have sent food."

"You can serve the ham and the coffee cake this afternoon. I can't eat anything now." Linda's eyes went back to the newspaper. The story about Lorna was not under Mike Marlowe's byline. Ed Sheely had written it. And on the same page was another story, with no byline at all. It was headed LORNA— ANOTHER LOOK.

With deepening horror she read, "Lorna Meyers, victim of Monday's sex murder, may not always have been so quiet. A person who knew her as a teenager remembers her as 'lively,' 'attractive,' and 'bold.'"

Blackness swam in front of her. She dropped the paper and put her head in her hands. Michael Marlowe! How could he? And he didn't even have the *guts* to sign his name to it.

"Linda! What's the matter?" Her aunt's voice brought her back.

"I ... I'm all right, Aunt Liz. Will you pour me another cup of coffee?"

While her aunt's back was turned, Linda fought for control of nausea and faintness. She picked up the paper. Although "Lorna—Another Look" did not have Michael Marlowe's byline, it had to be his work. He'd written all the stories about Lorna's death. His story on Tuesday, which began, "A quiet, gentle girl—" had almost brought her buried grief to the surface.

Now this. Where had Michael Marlowe gotten that description? He had interviewed someone who had known Lorna long ago. And he had betrayed her. She had looked into his blue eyes and seen sympathy and sincerity. She'd believed him when he promised that he would not twist Lorna's personality and her humiliating death into a sensational story.

When the police had come to tell her about Lorna's death, she had instantly consigned all men to hell. Then Uncle Henry had been a rock. The detective, García, who asked her about Lorna, had been gentle and tactful. Even Pastor Schmidt, whose pious utterances had no meaning for her, had been there and helped her make decisions about Lorna's funeral.

She had hated the hordes of media people with their bright lights and their crude, violent questions until Michael Marlowe's quiet tact had reminded her that they weren't all like that.

They were honest! They were openly, crassly out to get a story from her. He had tricked her, insinuated himself into her confidence, and made her trust him. To a grief so deep she could hardly acknowledge it and a rage that would never burn out, she now added loathing of Michael Marlowe.

She turned the paper to another page. She would never read another word about Lorna.

Ricky Foster's little face grinned. "Where Is This Child?" In her grief she had hardly thought of the parents of the little boy who had so completely and mysteriously disappeared in the wake of Lorna's death. She ought to write the Fosters a note, even try to see them. They were the only people in the world who could really understand. Their lives had been broken by the same tragedy.

Perhaps it was worse for them. She knew that Lorna's suffering was over, but they might never know what had happened to Ricky. For the rest of their lives...

She turned another page. Here again was the artist's drawing García had shown her, the man someone had seen near Lorna in the park. The face was featureless, marked only by glasses and a beard and a thick head of hair. He could be anybody. She knew she had never seen him.

García had asked her over and over again for details of Lorna's job, her relationship with the Fosters, names of fellow students at Columbia. The detective could not understand how quiet Lorna was, how little she talked about herself.

Lorna, Lorna... was there something I didn't know?

She closed the newspaper and folded it. "Aunt Liz, it's time to get ready."

"I know," her aunt said sadly.

THIRTEEN

SHE'D TRIED to take care of him. The Lord knew how she'd tried. But Billie was a skinny little thing, and he cried so much.

She'd always been alone. No one to help her with him. Billie's daddy was a soldier. She'd met him that summer night when they were painting Times Square red, white, and blue. She was just a kid then, on her first trip downstate. Once she saw New York, she never wanted to go back again.

Sometimes now when she was on her way to Port Authority, she went through Times Square and remembered how it glowed and rang that night—sirens and bells and whistles and the shouts of all those happy people.

And the soldier she met was so glad he didn't have to go over there and die. She'd never been sorry the way they celebrated that night even though she never saw him again.

When Billie came she'd taken him upstate and stayed with her folks for a few months. But they were ashamed of her. They were always sighing and wiping their eyes, and they tried to make the neighbors believe her "husband" had been killed in the war.

So she and Billie came back to New York on the train. At first it had been all right. Her folks, glad to see her go, had given her a little money. She found a rooming house where the landlady didn't mind kids, even looked after Billie for her when she had a job for a while. But she lost the job and things went from bad to worse.

That was when Billie began to cry so much she couldn't stand it. She found out that if she gave him cough syrup, it kept him quiet. Once she even put his little head into the gas oven—not enough to hurt him, but just to make him sleepy. That didn't work too good. When he came out of it, he threw up all over the place. Then he started crying and wouldn't stop. He got on her nerves so much that she cried herself and sometimes she screamed.

That's when she started hitting him. It was the only way to teach him that he mustn't cry. But he did anyway, a low, never-ending whine that scraped her nerves raw.

After a while she found an easy way to make money and sometimes she and Billie ate real good. But her landlady spied and threw them out. She took a room in a hotel. But when Billie got bigger, he wouldn't go to sleep when she wanted him to, and her customers were put off by the kid standing up in the bed watching.

She couldn't remember exactly what happened then. She'd started giving him aspirin so he'd sleep. Then one night he wouldn't wake up. She'd started screaming and someone had called the cops and the ambulance.

That was the bad time. It was all blurred in her mind. Those people all said she was crazy—cops, doctors, people in white uniforms. Anyway, it had all happened a long time ago. And it didn't matter anymore.

All that mattered was that she'd got Billie back. It was a miracle. The Lord had done it. He'd given Billie back. The Lord had taken him away and now the Lord had given him back. All she wanted to do was sit here and hold her baby in her arms and praise the Lord.

She'd take care of him this time. She wouldn't let them take him away from her again.

FOURTEEN

IN THE SMALL LIVING ROOM people squeezed and jostled and murmured. Linda stood just inside the door. Her throat ached and her face was stiff from the effort of talking. So many people had come. So many shocked, sympathetic faces. So many hands to shake.

In the hope that the final rites would lend dignity to Lorna in her death, she had wanted the funeral to be quiet and solemn. It had not been. From the reporters with their cameras and microphones, to the contingent of police who were even now outside trying to separate the mourners from the thrill-seekers, it was harrowing and highly public.

She was numbly tired, sick of the furtive curiosity that underlay the sympathy on too many faces. She was ready to admit that she'd made a mistake. She should have taken Aunt Liz's advice about not having the funeral guests back to the apartment.

The service had been too long. Pastor Schmidt had concluded his sermon with a call to the difficult task of finding compassion for Lorna's killer. Linda had simply closed her mind at that point and let his words roll unheard over her head.

"I'm real sorry, Linda!" The plump woman in front of her had tears in her eyes. "Lorna was such a sweetheart! Remember when she and Annie was such friends? Always laughing and teasing the boys? An animal, he must be, to have—" Linda thought quickly. This was Carrie Braun, who had lived behind them in Brooklyn. Her daughter Annie had been Lorna's best friend.

Linda squeezed Carrie's hand. "It's hard to understand," she said. "Thank you for coming."

Carrie moved to the dining ell where Aunt Liz and her helpers were serving coffee and cake and sandwiches.

Another face looked into hers, a young face, and another hand reached. "You probably don't remember me. I'm Kathy Rosen. Lorna and I were friends in high school. She was a doll, a real angel."

Linda remembered the bouncy girl who had come to the apartment several times to study chemistry with Lorna. At the time she'd been glad that her shy sister had a friend who was so outgoing. She pressed Kathy's hand with real gratitude.

The next hand was cool and firm. "I'm Gertrude Simonson, Lorna's guidance counselor. I feel so bad, Miss Meyers. It was my recommendation that got Lorna her job with the Fosters. I told Pat Foster how mature and responsible Lorna was. When I think what happened because she took that job, I feel so awful!"

Linda was beginning to perspire. The room was so crowded, so close. "You mustn't feel that way," she said to Gertrude. "You're not responsible for the act of a sick, violent man!"

Gertrude was wiping her eyes when she moved away.

The man who took her place was a stranger. He had dark hair, slicked down, and his eyes were shadowed by the tinted lenses of stylish sunglasses. His mouth opened on a shy smile that was quickly suppressed. "My name's—" he mumbled so unintelligibly that she did not catch it. "I knew Lorna a long time ago...I'm real sorry what happened..." His voice was husky, and the hand that shook hers was clammy. She caught a whiff of an odor, a strongly scented aftershave, perhaps. His face was tan and smooth and slightly shiny.

"Linda!" Pastor Schmidt was calling to her over the crowd. She turned. He was shoving his way toward her. "You must have some coffee and something to eat."

"Later, Pastor. I really want to speak to everyone who's been kind enough to come."

And curious enough. And ghoulish enough. If Lorna had died of pneumonia, would all these people be here? So many of them she did not know, like the man who had known Lorna a long time ago, whose name she did not hear. He was moving away now, not to the refreshments, but back out the door. Whoever he was, he had come only to pay his respects, not to eat.

To get out, the stranger had to push past a man who was just coming in, a man with light hair, whose eyes looked into hers as his hands reached out. "I had to come, Miss Meyers."

She snatched her hands back. "How did you get in here? I said no reporters!"

"I didn't come as a reporter. I came as a friend."

"A trick so you can feed your readers another sensation? Get out before I call a policeman to throw you out!" She was trying to keep her voice down, but its intensity brought several heads to turn in their direction.

Michael Marlowe's face had whitened. "Miss Meyers, I did not write that story."

She would not look at him again. He stood for a moment, then turned and was gone, shoving his way out the door he had just come in.

After that she hardly knew what she said to the people who still squeezed in. She mouthed her gratitude. More sad, concerned faces, more hands clasping hers.

Mercifully, it finally ended. The apartment emptied. Aunt Liz came into the living room from the kitchen, wiping her hands on her apron. "Are you sure you want to be alone tonight, Linda? I know you said so, but it doesn't seem right to me. Come back with us, stay a few days. Give yourself time."

"I have to start getting used to it right now, Aunt Liz. Monday I'm going back to work."

"She's right, Liz," said Henry Meyers. "The best thing to do is get back to a normal routine as soon as possible."

Her aunt was still doubtful. "Well, you certainly won't have to cook for a while. There's food for a week out there. I've put a lot of it in the freezer."

When the door closed behind her aunt and uncle, Linda had to stifle her dismay. Pastor Schmidt was still there, settled comfortably in a corner of the couch. Although she dreaded the moment when she would be alone, she did not want to talk to Schmidt. She sat down, swallowing a sigh.

"I overheard what you said to Michael Marlowe, Linda," he said with reproof in his voice. "When he interviewed me the other night, he impressed me with his sincerity."

"He took me in, too, Pastor. Did you see what he wrote about Lorna today?"

"I don't read the *Courier*, Linda," Schmidt said with faint distaste. "All I know is that Marlowe expressed a strong wish to help identify Lorna's killer. I hoped that the information I gave him would be helpful."

Sudden suspicion made her look at him hard. "What did you tell him about Lorna?"

"That she had a warm and—ah, fun-loving—personality when she was a youngster in Luther League. I stressed her regular attendance at worship, of course, and her strong faith at the time she was confirmed. I'll never forget how sincerely Lorna accepted my counsel. I know she believed in the Lord's mercy. You, Linda, must do the same."

Linda bowed her head. It was true. Pastor Schmidt was the source. Michael Marlowe had twisted Schmidt's naive and well-meaning comments about Lorna into a suggestive and sensational story. She had thought her loathing had reached its depth; now she knew it was bottomless.

She was silent. She'd been grateful for Schmidt's support at first; now she was sick with the realization of what he had done.

After a long silence he said, "Lorna believed in the Lord's mercy. She took her burdens to him in prayer. Before you try to rest tonight, Linda, you should do the same. Let his grace be sufficient for you."

It was all she could do to keep from putting her hands over her ears. She could stand no more of his inane and practiced pieties. At last her unresponsiveness got through to him; he rose and left.

The dreaded moment had come. She was alone in the apartment she'd shared with Lorna. What was she going to do with the hours that stretched before her until Monday when she could go back to work? She felt as if she would never sleep again. Down the hall was the closed door of Lorna's room. Behind it her clothes, her books, her records, her loved possessions like the locket Mom had left her. All would have to be sorted, packed, given away.

It would be months before she could even open that door.

Lorna, I didn't know you!

For a second her buried anguish broke through. Lorna, a little girl with a mop of brown curls, happy and chattering with excitement when her big sister took her to the corner store and bought her ice cream. And after Daddy and Mom were gone, Lorna, the quiet, dependable teenager who always had dinner ready for her when she came home from work.

Somewhere during those hard years, she had lost Lorna.

Now she had lost her forever.

Someday, if she could bring herself to talk to Pastor Schmidt again, she'd ask him why he'd had to counsel Lorna. Most likely it was to comfort her and help her to accept those two deaths.

Oh, Lorna, in those last dreadful moments, did you call on your Lord? Did he spare you the full horror? Lorna had been unconscious, or nearly so, the medical examiner had reported.

Oh, God, let it be so! That would be mercy, all the mercy Linda Meyers would ever pray for.

She bowed her head and put her hands over her face. Prayer would not come. Neither would tears. Her eyes were still dry and her throat still tight a few minutes later when she got up and went over to her desk. She took out a sheet of stationery and a pen.

"Dear Mr. and Mrs. Foster," she wrote. "My heart goes out to you in this terrible time. My sister is beyond pain now, but you have to live with not knowing. When we are strong enough to bear it, I would like to meet you. People who share the same tragedy should know one another. Who else can understand? With sincere sympathy, Linda Meyers."

FIFTEEN

PAT FOSTER'S FACE was taut, her eyes deeply shadowed. Beside her, her husband Rowland looked like a man stiff with horror as he felt himself bleeding to death from an internal wound.

If they were faking, they were doing a hell of a good job.

"We ask anyone who has any information about our son, please call the police at this number—" Rowland said as the number appeared on the screen below the two seated figures.

When Pat's turn came, she looked right into the camera. It was like she was looking right at him. Her voice was clear and soft. "Ricky was wearing blue jeans, size three. A red-and-white striped shirt and a navy blue jacket. Blue sneakers. He had his blanket with him. He takes it with him wherever he goes."

Her control failed her for an instant. She glanced away from the camera. Then her eyes came back. "The blanket is blue, with a satin binding." She swallowed. "Whoever you are, you have no reason to fear an innocent child, no reason to harm him."

Bullshit!

Robert Lawrence Orsine snapped off the TV. It was a trap. Ricky was snug in his crib on 92nd Street off Central Park West. The police had got these two to go in front of the cameras and act like people who would do anything to get their kid back. What did they expect? Someone to write a ransom note and ask for a suitcase full of thousand-dollar bills? A suitcase all wired up so whoever picked it up could be tracked down?

He switched the TV on again. The Fosters had finished their pitch. The silent image of two anguished faces remained on the screen for a second, then it faded.

Suppose they were on the level. Suppose the kid really was missing. Then where the fuck was he?

The anchorman was repeating the plea for information. A reward was offered. The police number was on the screen again.

Orsine turned off the TV for good.

He was fucking around in his mind again, the way he'd done three days ago. He was sick with uncertainty. He'd had his chance to grab Ricky Foster, to make sure, but he blew it.

Now he had to know where that kid was. He had to find out. He knew he could get away with almost anything after the cool way he'd walked into Linda's apartment this afternoon and shook her hand. He hadn't gone to the funeral. At the last minute he knew he couldn't do that. But he'd gone to the apartment.

Just as he'd put his hand to Linda, he'd had a horrible thought. How much had Lorna told her sister? He'd broken into a sweat. Linda looked enough like Lorna to make him feel real crazy.

Then he'd almost keeled over. Pastor Schmidt was pushing his way through the crowd. Just in the nick of time he'd realized that the "disguise" that made him unrecognizable as the man the cops were after wouldn't serve him here. His beard had been nothing but fuzz ten years ago, and he'd worn his hair combed down like it was now.

Surely Linda didn't recognize him. She'd never seen that much of him. She came to church only now and then. And she was never friendly like Lorna.

Lorna was the only girl in the church who was halfway decent to him. The other kids made fun of him because he was so big and had such a hard time saying things that were smart and funny. But Lorna liked him anyway. She was always smiling at him. She smiled at all the boys, but he knew she thought he was special. She was always moving her body in ways that sent the heat into his brain and the stiffness into him that was so hard to hide.

He could stiffen now, just thinking of her.

He had to stop this. He must not remember that night. She'd been so willing to go with him. Her eyes had looked sorry and she'd said "OK, Bobby," in that sweet way when he told her he wanted to talk to her. She knew what he wanted. She wanted it, too.

Stop this, Orsine!

He had to go on thinking about himself. He was in terrible danger, but he was doing real good so far. He'd been smart enough to duck out this afternoon when he realized Schmidt might recognize him. He'd been smart enough to get himself a free meal at his sisters' house as long as he was in the neighborhood.

He opened the paper. There was a police artist's picture of the suspect. All hair and beard and glasses. Like a cartoon. Like a little kid's drawing of a man.

By God, that's just what it was! Orsine laughed out loud. His hunch was right. The cops had given Ricky Foster a pencil and told him to draw a picture of the man who'd made a wabbit for him. Then the artist had put on the finishing touches.

He didn't look anything like this now. No one would connect him with that fathead in the blue suit. And hardly anyone would connect him with Lorna. His sister Barbara hadn't even mentioned Lorna's death.

When he got his hair cut, he'd look real good. Short on the back and sides was the new macho image. Maybe Lorna would have liked him better if—

He squeezed his eyes shut. He would not think about her, not see her in his head the way she looked laying there, her eyes staring, her legs—

He'd get his hair cut tomorrow. He'd go back to work. The boss was mad that he'd called in sick three days in a row. He'd have the whole weekend to snoop around, see what he could pick up.

SIXTEEN

THE CAMERA CREW was gone. Husband and wife still sat side by side on the couch where they'd been taped delivering their plea for Ricky. The front room, a shambles now with telephone cables and all the paraphernalia of a police inquiry center, was, for the first time since Monday night, empty except for themselves.

"It isn't really blue anymore. It's almost gray. How could I have forgotten that?" Tears spilled out of Pat's eyes.

Her husband spoke stiffly, hardly moving his mouth. "And you a 'painter'!" He managed to convey contempt, not only for her, but for the whole art world.

She had to remember that Rowland was beside himself with fear, and fear made him rigid. His whole body was stiff. He moved his head toward her slowly, as if to relax his muscles for a second meant to relax his vigilance. And if he relaxed his vigilance, Ricky would be gone forever.

She wanted to fling her body wildly, to run, to move, even to dance to express her terrible panic and her even worse guilt.

"You wanted to be 'creative.' You wanted to smear paint on canvas and call yourself an artist. Being a good wife and mother wasn't enough for you." Rowland's monotone had taken on the quality of an incantation. He couldn't bear the anguish and suspense. He was holding it at bay by forcing guilt on her.

Their marriage had been a risk for both of them. It could break over this.

The buttoned-up young lawyer in his three-piece suit had come to the SoHo gallery, dragged to her opening by friends, and so out of his element that he was shocked by the boldness of her canvases.

He was fascinated, too, and he had so far forgotten himself that he asked her out to dinner.

Rowland had old-fashioned ideas about relationships. His persistence was flattering. She, too, forgot herself, forgot that she'd wanted to live only for painting. They were married a few months after they'd met.

Their differences in temperament and interests had been something to laugh about, and as Rowland had unbent, she'd tried to be more conforming. Ricky's birth had brought them as close as they'd ever been.

Now they were falling apart.

Fear for his son had driven Rowland into a rigidity which held not only his body, but his mind, in a vise. He had to lash out at her or go insane. She was losing Rowland. She had lost Ricky.

Two days and three nights. So little chance he was still alive—if he was in the park. No food, no water, no arms to hold him close. Her little boy—frightened and alone.

If he wasn't in the park—

She felt herself go as rigid as Rowland. Her mind tried to veer off. She knew what Detective García thought had happened to Ricky. He didn't say it in front of her, but she knew what he was thinking. Every day, children were swallowed up in a vicious traffic in young bodies.

The psychopath who had killed Lorna had taken her little boy. She would never see him again.

Rowland's voice brought her back from the unbearable agony. "If you had to leave him, why didn't you employ a nanny from a reliable agency? A mature person with good references?"

"Lorna wasn't an irresponsible teenager. She was mature, and she had excellent references. You read them yourself, Rowland."

This conversation had become a litany. They'd had it, it seemed, every few hours since Monday night.

"You should have seen that the girl meant trouble," Rowland said suddenly.

"How on earth would I have seen that?" This was a new point in the case Rowland was making against her.

"She was so pretty. She had to have men in her life."

Lorna? Pretty? Yes, the girl had been pretty in a well-scrubbed way. Beautiful bones. Clear skin, eyes with remarkable lashes, and a mass of light brown hair strained back severely.

"But not seductive, surely, Rowland?" Pat pleaded. "Her clothes were nondescript, she didn't wear makeup. If she was conscious of her looks, she certainly didn't flaunt them."

"True, there was something nunlike about her."

Pat relaxed slightly. Rowland agreed with her. That was something. She remembered the day he'd come home just as Lorna and Ricky came in from the park. At the time she'd wondered if he had left work early to see for himself the sitter she'd hired. He'd had no complaints about Lorna then. And none about Pat's painting beyond an amused comment or two.

Ricky didn't need a nanny. Rowland knew as well as she did that she could take care of him herself. All she wanted were those few hours every day. She didn't call herself an artist, she *was* an artist. She had to get back to her painting or die. She'd cleaned out the extra bedroom and set up her easel. She'd called the placement office at Columbia for the names of students who'd registered for baby-sitting.

Ricky loved Lorna. It was good for him, too, not to be with his mother all day long.

The irony brought fresh pain, more than she could bear without moving. She left the couch where Rowland sat, stiff and silent in his misery. She went over to the high windows that faced north on 92nd Street and stood behind the curtains, clinging to them so as not to be seen from the street. She looked over at the trees in the park.

Ricky, where are you?

Below, people still waited on the street and on the sidewalk. Some with cameras and microphones. Some merely curious and interested. A few police, men and women, to see that the normal traffic of the street and building were not impeded.

She watched one of their first-floor tenants go down the steps. Reporters surged forward briefly, then fell back when they recognized her. She was a person who gave them nothing.

Pat looked again at the trees. Some were already bare and others still had the brown and gold of autumn clinging to them.

The sky arched deep and blue above the trees. She couldn't bear it. She had to go out there under those trees and be where Ricky had been.

She watched as Hanna in her bright head scarf and dark glasses walked briskly to the corner of Central Park West.

SEVENTEEN

THE WOMAN'S HAIR was drawn back under a bright silk scarf which contrasted sharply with the pallor of her face. She wore blue jeans and a brown sweater and sneakers. She was sitting on a bench in a blaze of October sunshine, watching the children who swarmed over the climbing structures, slides, and swings. Beside her on the bench was a leather purse. On top of it was a pair of sunglasses and a child's toy truck.

Pat Foster.

Mike could hardly believe his luck. He slowed his approaching footsteps. What was she doing out here in the park alone? He looked around for escorting cops, but he saw none. How had she managed to get out of her apartment without being followed? Media people still hovered in front of the building, shouting questions at police, tenants, and visitors as they went in and out.

Lorna Meyers' death was yesterday's news, but Ricky Foster's disappearance was still hot.

"Mrs. Foster?"

In the brown eyes that looked at him, he saw first alarm and then defeat. She put on the glasses and got up.

"Please don't go! I'm Michael Marlowe. I only want to tell you how sorry I am. I'd like to help you."

"Marlowe? Michael Marlowe? Aren't you a reporter?"

"No, I'm not. Not anymore."

"What are you talking about?" She was taking long, angry strides. Mike kept pace with her.

"I'm no longer with the *Courier*. My editor and I disagreed about the way the story should be covered."

She stopped. "What does that have to do with me?"

"I have a personal reason to find out who killed Lorna Meyers and who took your little boy."

"What possible personal reason could you have except for a story with your name on it?"

"Lorna Meyers."

"You? You were involved with Lorna? Do the police know?"

"Not Lorna. Her sister Linda." If he succeeded in finding the killer, he hoped God would forgive him for putting hope before truth.

"How do I know this isn't a trick? Yesterday a reporter bribed a market delivery boy to let him bring in our groceries. He was in our kitchen taking pictures. We had to get the police to throw him out."

Mike reached inside his jacket and took out his notebook. He scribbled a name and number and handed it to her. "This is my editor. Call him and ask if Mike Marlowe still works for the *Courier*. He'll tell you I quit on Tuesday."

She took the paper and looked at it. Then she handed it back to him. "What makes you think you can help me? What can you do that the police can't?"

This time he could tell her only the truth. "I have to do something."

She took off the glasses. Her brown eyes, ringed with deep circles, looked steadily into his. Then she said, "I'll give you a few minutes, that's all. And if this is a trick—"

"It's not, I promise you." He'd made Linda a promise, too, and now he had her contempt.

When they were back at the bench, she took the toy truck in her hands and held it tightly.

He'd gained this much of her trust. He had to make it work. To put her at ease he said, "I'm surprised you could get out of your apartment without being seen."

"The woman who lives downstairs is near my size and coloring. She's been in and out so often without talking to the media that they've stopped asking her. I told her I was going crazy imprisoned like that, and she let me borrow her scarf and glasses. They thought I was her. I walked right past."

"Why did you come here?"

"Why did you?"

"This seemed the place to start."

"It's the same for me," she said after a small pause. "I thought if I could be here where he was last seen, I'd notice something, feel something, that the police couldn't know. I'm his mother. I ought to *feel* it if he's still alive."

"Do you? Do you know anything you didn't when you were a prisoner in your apartment waiting for the phone to ring?"

She looked around before she answered. "I see autumn in the park. Leaves are falling. Children are playing. Their mothers are loving them. And I'm loving Ricky, and I don't know if he's alive or dead."

Mike reached for his notebook. Then he checked himself. He was not a reporter now. He was Pat Foster's friend and ally, and he needed her help. "Tell me everything you know about Lorna."

"I told Detective García everything, every scrap I could remember."

"Tell it again. Something may come up for you that didn't before. I only know what I read in the *Courier*. She'd been sitting for you for a month, is that right?"

"Five weeks. When I wanted some free time during the day, I called the placement office at Columbia for the names of sitters. Lorna was the first one I interviewed."

"How many interviews did you have with her?"

"Only one. She was exactly the person I was looking for, and Ricky took to her right away. Both her references—her high school guidance counselor and a woman she'd worked for in Queens—said she was completely dependable."

"She was a lively girl, wasn't she? I suppose that's why she was so good with kids?"

Pat looked shocked. "Oh, no! Lorna wasn't like that at all. She was just the opposite. Very quiet. Almost grave."

Something stirred in the back of Mike's mind. That strange contradiction again. "You had no problems with her?"

"None. Ricky adored her. She had a gift for treating small children with dignity. Ricky jabbered about 'Worna' this and 'Worna' that."

"Did your husband ever meet her?"

"Only once. I'm afraid Rowland will never forgive himself. Or me. Now he thinks I should have known that Lorna meant trouble—she was so pretty." Pat put down the toy truck and fumbled in her purse for a tissue.

"Your husband's terribly frightened. When he's had time to think, surely he won't be so unreasonable. He's a lawyer, isn't he?"

"That's not all of it, Mister Marlowe." She wiped her eyes.

"Please call me Mike."

"Mike. Thank you." Words began to pour out of her now, words she'd been holding in. "I think this must be God's punishment on me. I wanted time to paint. I wanted something for myself, something besides husband and child. Now God's taken my baby away!"

"I don't believe in that kind of God. I don't think you do either."

A screech of wheels became audible even from this distance. They watched the woman in layers of shapeless, dirty clothes as she pushed a deep shopping cart along the walk on the other side of the playground. While Pat wiped her face and tried to get herself under control, Mike kept his eyes on the old woman who stopped every once in a while to wave her arms. She seemed to be singing. On a light gust of wind her voice came over the children's shouts. "Praise the Lord! Praise him in his temple!"

"Poor old soul! Poor lost old soul!" Pat cried.

"I don't know," said Mike. "She doesn't look awfully un-happy to me." Indeed, the bag lady's seamed face wore an expression of manic glee.

"Maybe she has all she wants in life," Pat said sadly.

"Tell me what Ricky and Lorna did when she was in charge of him." He wanted to get Pat's mind off the bag lady and back to the little boy's disappearance.

"Lorna came every day at twelve-thirty," Pat began. She spoke automatically, as if she had recited these facts often in the past few days. "If it rained, she played with him in the apartment. If the weather was nice, she brought him here." She nodded at the children on the swings and slides. "I—that is Rowland and I—want Ricky to play with other children, especially children of other backgrounds."

When she did not go on, Mike asked, "Was there any particular child he played with?"

"A little girl named Robin Ruiz. Her mother, Jeanette, called the police when she heard about the dead girl. But García says she hasn't been able to tell them anything helpful. I was hoping to see her myself today, but there's no one on the playground who looks like the people García described. She's a small woman, Hispanic, very light-skinned, he said, and the little girl has curly hair."

"What else did Lorna and Ricky do?"

"Sometimes they watched a ball game."

"Did Lorna ever mention meeting anyone in the park, besides Robin and her mother? Did Ricky?"

"No one but 'Wobin' and Mister Boo. Rowland thinks Lorna was meeting a man. Maybe this Mister Boo. Detective García won't tell us anything about him. But I can't believe that Lorna would do anything irresponsible. She was pretty, but she wasn't at all sexy. Even Rowland admitted she was nunlike."

"Did Ricky say anything about this Mister Boo?"

"He chatters so. I know I don't listen as I should. All I can remember is that Ricky said that Mr. Boo gave him a ride."

"A ride? How—piggyback? On a bicycle?"

Pat's head was down. The tears were falling again. "Don't you know how many times I've told myself I should have paid attention to his chatter? Asked questions? I should know!"

"Did Lorna ever mention this Mister Boo?"

"Not a word. She and I had very little conversation. She brought Ricky home at five and gave him a bath. I stopped my work at five-thirty. Lorna never said much more than 'He was a really good boy today,' or 'We have fun, don't we Ricky?' Then she said goodbye."

"Tell me about Ricky. I know very little about two year olds. I suppose he walks?"

She dried her eyes and smiled slightly. "He runs most of the time. Lorna takes—took—him in the stroller so he could have a little nap on the way home. Otherwise he's cranky at suppertime. Ricky's small for his age, but he's well coordinated."

"He talks? Not just baby talk?"

"He's very articulate for two. He counts. He knows all the colors. He speaks short sentences and he speaks clearly except for *L* and *R*. He called her 'Worna.'"

Pat's face, which had become animated and almost normal in color, froze suddenly as her gaze shifted over Michael's shoulder. He turned around. He had never seen the man except in his TV plea, but he recognized Rowland Foster.

Ricky's father was striding toward them, followed by a phalanx of reporters and a couple of cops. His face was white. "I don't know who you are, but you get away from my wife!"

"Rowland, it's all right. This is Michael Marlowe. He's been talking with me, not as a reporter but as a friend."

"Like hell! You're too gullible for your own good, Pat. For *our* own good! What if the kidnapper calls and wants to speak to you? And you out here running around in the park where no one can find you?"

Pat stood up quickly. She put on the dark glasses and tied the scarf around her now colorless face. She held out her hand to Mike. "If you find out anything, Mr. Marlowe..."

"I'll let you know."

"There's nothing he can find out that the police don't already know," said Rowland. "Come along, Pat."

Mike watched the husband and wife walk away. They were side by side but did not touch each other. Both stared straight ahead.

Ed Sheely had separated himself from the reporters who were trailing the Fosters. His face was full of resentment. "What the hell are you up to, Marlowe?"

"I'm not trying to get my job back, if that's what you're worried about. I didn't find out a damn thing."

But he had. The police were keeping quiet about a mystery man Ricky had called Mister Boo. That was a mere puzzle compared to the real mystery, the one that would not go away.

Lorna Meyers. Who had described the real Lorna—her sister Linda and her employer Pat?

Or Pastor Schmidt?

EIGHTEEN

LOUISE HOBBLED BEHIND her cart. Her feet were swollen. She struggled because she was in a hurry. The late afternoon sunshine slanted sharply across the street, and already the day had lost its warmth.

She needed that whisky now. She could feel it in her throat already, burning and glowing.

She'd give Billie a sip. He'd been a good boy. Not a peep out of him all day. The cough syrup had done its trick again!

This was her lucky day. The drunk in the doorway hadn't even stirred when she'd snatched up his half-full bottle. She'd tucked it into the cart. All day she'd savored in anticipation the lovely moment. Soon.

This was the hardest block, the longest one. Uphill all the way to Amsterdam along Cathedral Parkway. She'd often thought of finding a place closer to the park. There was a real palace at the corner of 106th Street. It was all boarded up, but she could find a way to get in.

The big problem was that the park was too far away from food. She had restaurants along Broadway where the trash could be counted on, and markets where she could pick up overripe fruit and discarded produce. She even knew proprietors who felt sorry for her and looked the other way when she popped this and that into the deep pockets of her coat.

She also knew places to sit and wait for a handout. Not that she would beg! Never! She had too much pride and self-respect. She wasn't like old Gus, who shared the building with her. He hung around the subway platform with his pants falling off and asked people for change. She'd never do that. She always blessed the folks who gave her money. She bought herself treats. A hero, sometimes, or a slice.

Billie would love pizza!

The cathedral steps was the best place, even though the fucking security guards were always making her move along. People who came out of the cathedral were usually pretty generous—the Lord had moved them.

What was she thinking of, moving closer to the park? She couldn't do that, she'd be too far from the cathedral! She often sneaked in, tagging along with those big groups of tourists so the busybodies at the information desk didn't see her. She'd slip down a side aisle and lift the rope that kept sinners away from the high altar. She'd sneak into a high, cushioned pew in the choir and sleep, sheltered and safe. At the far end, high up, the Lord glowed in the great blue window.

Sometimes the organ started playing while she was there. She knew where to hide so she was out of the organist's sight if he looked down from his bench. When he played, the huge place reverberated with rolling, pounding waves of sound. Sometimes, wakened up that way, she thought she'd died and gone to heaven.

At the corner of Morningside Drive she had to stop. The old heart was beating too hard and the blood was singing in her head. She leaned heavily on the handle of the cart.

"Hey, Lou! Look here a minute!" A young cop was grinning at her from the rolled-down window of the patrol car that had stopped for the light.

"Bug off, smart ass!" Her heart lurched. He was going to ge' out of that cop car and look in her cart.

They were looking for Billie. His picture was taped up all over the place. The cops had gone through every building on every street this side of the park. Yesterday she'd seen the patrol cars, seen the blue uniforms scurrying like rats in and out of buildings and stores, turning over stuff in vacant lots. She'd waited till she was sure they were gone before she slipped back in to her place.

"We're looking for a lost kid, Lou. The one in that picture. Ricky Foster is his name. You seen him?"

"Go fuck yourself!" They were trying to trick her.

The cop laughed. "Same old Lou! Watcha got in the cart, Lou, a picnic lunch?"

She reached into the top of the cart and pulled out the bottle. She showed her blackened teeth in what she hoped was a knowing grin.

"Was I right or wasn't I?" the cop laughed, looking over at his partner. "Have a ball, Lou!"

When the car moved on up Cathedral Parkway, she almost peed in her pants. That was close. She slipped the bottle back into the cart, and her fingers touched the silky hair on Billie's head.

"Missing" was printed on the picture on the light post right beside her. Billie's face grinned at her.

She laughed out loud. Billie wasn't missing. Praise the Lord! Billie was right where he belonged.

NINETEEN

POLICE QUIZ NEW SEX CRIME SUSPECTS the headline blared. Mike almost tore the late edition apart.

He read quickly. Walt Edwin and Jim Kent, both age nineteen, had been playing ball on the field next to the murder site. They were not with the four who had found and reported the body. They had left the field ahead of the rest of their team.

Mike had to find out. His decision the other day had cost him his sources. The encounter with Pat had been pure luck. An interview with García would require some inventiveness on his part. Or he could swallow his pride and call Ed Sheely.

He decided to try García, on the hope that the detective did not know he'd left the paper. At the Central Park police station he met García just coming out. Mike introduced himself. The detective looked puzzled. "I remember you," he said. "You were here Monday night. Someone else has been asking questions for the *Courier* since then."

"Ed and I are working from different angles," Mike said. "He's covering both the murder and the kidnapping in detail, and I'm doing sort of an overview. Tell me what these new suspects—Edwin and Kent—have to do with Ricky?"

"I'm on my way over to the Fosters. I'll talk with you if you want to walk along."

Mike fell into step. The detective's feet were coming down hard on the pavement, almost as if he were stamping out his anger.

"Ricky Foster has been the object of the biggest search for a missing kid in this city in years," García said. "We've talked with hundreds of people who were in the park Monday and hundreds who weren't. We're following up every phone call, and they're coming in by the dozen. We've questioned drunks and junkies and derelicts. We've covered every square foot of this park, dragged every body of water, opened every sewer and climbed down every fucking manhole. The kid is not in the park, dead or alive.''

"How about all those rocks and crevices up in the north end?''

"Hell, we didn't leave so much as a dead leaf unturned!''

"No one has contacted the Fosters for ransom?''

"You're covering the story. You know that.''

"The police might not want the press to know everything.''

"What's that supposed to mean?''

"You tell me. What's the official story on Ricky Foster?''

"I'll tell you that when you tell me how a kid disappeared into thin air in broad daylight.''

"When his baby-sitter didn't come back, he climbed out of the stroller and wandered over to the playground. He started playing with a bunch of kids, tagged along when they went home.''

"You mean some woman comes to the park with kids of her own and takes home an extra one? You're fantasizing because you've got no facts. Use your brains, Marlowe! It was raining then, raining hard. Everyone had gone home. There wasn't anyone left on the playground after five o'clock Monday afternoon.''

"Someone hanging around, then,'' Mike continued stubbornly. "A woman who wants a baby so badly she'll take someone else's. Like the ones who steal babies from hospital nurseries. I covered a story on that once.''

The detective nodded glumly. "It's a possibility. Anyone who took a stray kid knows by this time he's Ricky Foster and that there's a reward for him. Someone may have wanted a kid badly, but not for the reason you'd like to think.''

"I know. If he was taken by accident or for ransom or frustrated maternal feelings, it has to be a pederast or the kid porn producers.''

"We haven't found a single person who remembers seeing anyone—man or woman—with a child in an unusual situation. Only parents and sitters rushing kids home when the rain started. We've questioned cabbies. People at bus stops and on subway platforms. We think now that whoever took him had a car parked on Central Park West. A van maybe. Got the kid into it unseen and took off."

"The killer?"

"Maybe not. Maybe two separate crimes. Someone rapes the girl and kills her and runs. Someone else finds the kid alone and snatches him."

"Who's Mister Boo?"

García's face lost its furrowed, simian misery and became furious. "What the hell do you know about him?"

"Ricky came home from the park and chattered to his mother about a man he called Mister Boo. Sounds like Lorna *was* meeting a man in the park."

"Reporters!" García tramped on.

"Who's Mister Boo?"

"How did you find out about him?"

"Pat Foster told me. I met her by accident here this morning. I know what she told me was off the record. My guess is that Mister Boo is either a witness or a suspect, and that you've got a good reason for concealing him from the press. I don't want to put anything in the paper that would be useful to the killer or the kidnapper. That's why I wanted to talk to you." Mike was beginning to sweat. He was spinning a tangle of lies that could cost him García's candor.

They were crossing the West Drive now. A gaggle of runners went by. Both men looked automatically. Shorts, T-shirts, one red sweatsuit, one gray. No blue. No beard.

They descended into the hollow and approached the comfort station. Mike wondered if García had brought him this way for a reason.

"Stay here a minute," said the detective. "I want to check something out."

He walked to the far side of the structure and ducked behind the shrubs and low trees that edged the weedy space. "Can you see me?" he called.

"Yes."

"How much?"

"Only your legs. The rest is hidden by branches."

"What about my face?"

"Just enough to know you're looking at me."

García pushed the branches aside and came back. "Look at that!" he exclaimed bitterly. He pointed to the hedge screening the chain-link fence along the ballfield. The twigs were almost bare, and the field was clearly visible. "Four days ago you couldn't see this sidewalk from that field, those leaves were so thick. The wind and rain the night of the murder brought most of them down."

Even as García spoke, a gust of wind flung more leaves pattering to the ground from the branches over their heads. Mike said, "You mean if it happened today, he wouldn't get away with it? Someone would have seen her dragged in here? I still wonder why no one heard her scream."

"She didn't."

"Why not?"

"She didn't want to scare the kid. Then the killer put his hand over her mouth. There was blood on her teeth. She bit him. We have his blood analysis."

"There could be another reason she didn't scream."

"She knew him? The press has tried to make something of that, but her sister is so insistent Lorna wasn't interested in men that I just don't buy it."

"Who's Mister Boo?"

"Let's sit down. I want to get some thing straight with you." García led the way out of the hollow to the benches near the playground. A blare of sound assaulted their ears. A youth with a radio the size of a suitcase on the bench beside him took one look at the detective and rose and slouched away. Mike and García took the seat he had vacated.

"Mister Boo," said García, "is Ricky's name for our sole witness, a man who supplied us with the description. We've dozens of reports about men in blue sweatsuits, but with the marathon coming up Sunday, guys in athletic gear are coming out of the shrubbery. This witness came forward, called us Tuesday. He said that twice he'd seen a bearded man in a blue suit. Once the guy ran past the girl and the kid when they were sitting near him on a bench. Then a few days later the same man sat down on a bench across from them. Stayed a couple of minutes, then jogged off. We're keeping this witness' identity from the media for his protection. OK, Marlowe—" García shifted position and faced Mike directly. "I've given you this. Now I want to know what you got from Pat."

Mike was very uncomfortable. "She didn't tell me anything beyond Ricky's name for the man because that's all she knows. The only other thing she could remember is that Ricky said the man had given him a ride."

"Humph." That was all García said.

"Is this description all you have?"

"Not quite. We now have a partial description from one of the men we questioned this morning, Walt Edwin."

"Partial?"

"Half a man. Legs in blue sweatpants."

"In the bushes there where you asked me what I could see? Edwin actually saw the guy?"

"Edwin and Kent left the field ahead of the rest of the team as soon as the game was called. They hollered that they were going over to Amsterdam to have a beer. They never went— we've talked to bartenders in every bar for blocks. A man at a bus stop on Central Park West told us he had seen those two running out of the park at about twenty past five, looking, in his words, 'scared shitless.' They ran across the avenue against traffic and disappeared into the apartment complex. This morning when we confronted them, we got absolute denial. They'd seen no child, no dead woman, no stroller, nothing. Finally we got an admission that they'd seen a stroller and a toy truck. Then Edwin claimed he'd seen a pair of legs in blue behind the bushes on the far side of the comfort station. That's what scared him so much he ran."

"What about the other man, Kent?"

"He says he saw nothing. When Edwin yelled 'Run!' he ran."

"What was so frightening about blue legs? The guy could have been taking a pee."

"That's where the story gets murky. Edwin says that there was something 'fucking weird, man,' about the scene. The abandoned toy and empty stroller, rain coming down harder and harder, someone watching them from the bushes. He just wanted to get the fuck out of there."

"You don't believe him."

"The description of a man in a blue sweatsuit has been in the paper since Tuesday."

"You think Edwin and Kent—"

"Hold it! All I said was they denied everything, and unless we find this guy in the blue suit or some other witness, we can't prove Edwin and Kent are lying."

"Was either of them bitten on the hand?"

"No."

"And that really pisses you off, doesn't it? You'd like to be able to pin this rape and murder on them, wouldn't you?"

"The hell I would! You're too smart, Marlowe, to jump to conclusions like that. You know what bad business it is to even hint that we suspect a black man of the rape and murder of a white woman. We've got to have an airtight case—witnesses, lab evidence, the works. Right now all we've got is circumstantial and very dubious evidence. And I don't want to see your name on any fucking crusade for Edwin and Kent."

"You won't see my name on anything."

"Why not?"

"I quit the paper."

García was on his feet. His sad eyes were blazing. "Then why are you wasting my time, for Christ's sake?"

"Personal interest." Mike stood up too. Words came out almost in spite of himself. He could tell this cop. It would be a relief to get it out. "My sister—she was only sixteen."

"Killed?"

"She wishes she had been."

"Did they arrest him?"

"She couldn't identify him—even if she could have stood what she would have had to go through in court. He was wearing a ski mask."

García nodded. "That's tough, Marlowe. I'm sorry. It explains why you're on your own damn crusade. I can't blame you even though I wish you weren't."

"I want to do something."

"Keep us informed."

"Of course!"

"And for God's sake be careful! And don't screw things up for us."

This might be the last chance to get any police information. He had to know two things. "Are you giving up on the man in the blue suit?"

"We're not 'giving up' on anything. But the evidence of only one witness isn't enough."

"And what about this Mister Boo? Seems to me he'd be your number one suspect."

García's response was a short, mirthless snort. "Not a fucking chance!"

After Mike separated from García, he continued across to Amsterdam. He walked uptown until he came to an Italian restaurant in the block below the Cathedral of St. John the Divine. Over a plate of spaghetti and a bottle of Michelob, he gloomily reviewed his information. He pulled out his notebook and jotted as he thought.

The assumption that the man in blue was rapist, killer, and kidnapper was not clear-cut. It was in fact fogged with uncertainty and supported by no evidence that would stand up in court.

Evidence that came from a witness who could himself be the chief suspect. Why was García so certain he was not? Mike scribbled a line of question marks after the name "Mister Boo." The man had given Ricky a ride. Did that mean wheels? Not necessarily. He'd thought of piggyback when he was talking with Pat.

Edwin and Kent. They'd run from a pair of blue legs in the bushes. Had they, unknowing, helped the killer get away?

Mike understood now why García was so angry. With no new clues to the murder, no trace of Ricky Foster, and the handful of meager facts dissolving as he looked at them, the chances of finding the killer and recovering the lost child grew dimmer with each passing hour.

Now García seemed to be doubting even the existence of the man in the blue sweatsuit.

Mike took a swallow of beer. The folly of his own situation was bitterly apparent to him. He had thrown away his job to embark on just what García had called it—a crusade. He had given in to an impulse which now seemed stupidly quixotic. He should have taken up his editor's offer of a few days to think it over. He'd been carried away by the emotions and memories the rape and murder of Lorna Meyers had aroused in him, and he had been sickened by what seemed callousness in his chosen profession.

Now Linda's fragile trust had turned to scorn. Instead of doing something positive, he had wounded her further. He would never have a chance to prove to her that he had not written "Lorna—Another Look."

He could go back to his editor and ask to be reinstated. He could start looking for another job. Neither alternative appealed to him.

He finished his beer and took a last look at the notes he'd made. "Edwin and Kent." "Mister Boo." A row of question marks. That was all he had for his grand gesture, a row of question marks.

And the biggest question of all was Lorna Meyers.

The only person he had not talked to yet was Jeanette Ruiz, the last name on his list. He'd go back to the park and look for her.

Outside the restaurant the pitiful old woman he'd seen in the park this morning was shuffling along the sidewalk behind her shopping cart. At the corner she stopped. Her eyes darted up and down the street. Then she plunged her hands into the trash basket chained to a light post on the corner. With something like triumph, she pulled out a cardboard half-pint milk container, upright, with a straw sticking out of it. She shook it; then angrily she threw it back into the trash.

Mike reached into his pocket. He fingered some bills. When he got to the corner where the old woman still rummaged, he slowed his steps.

She looked around. She clutched the handle of the shopping cart. "Go away! Leave me be!" Her dirty, lined face was convulsed.

Mike turned his back. He let the bills fall from his hand and he headed for the curb. He heard a rustle behind him. Then her voice sang out, "Bless you, sir! May the Lord bless you! Now Billie can have milk. That's what Billie wants—milk!"

Mike did not look back until he had crossed 112th Street. When he did, the old woman was nowhere in sight.

TWENTY

LOUISE SLID the rusty bolt. Safe!

Her room at the back of the stripped, cavernous building was dark and clammy. She scrabbled for the candle in a chipped saucer and lighted it. The boarded windows would not betray her presence to the street. Gus was the only one who knew. They shared this shelter. He wouldn't tell on her and she wouldn't tell on him.

Now Billie knew. This was his home. He was back home with his mommy.

She shivered even in her coat. It was getting so cold at night now. Soon they wouldn't be able to stay here. She could go downtown and hang around Grand Central or Port Authority like she had for so many winters she'd lost count. But what would she do with Billie? They'd be watching in those places, waiting for the chance to grab him, take him away from her again.

If only they could live in the cathedral. It had so many places he could hide. It had wash basins and toilets. Billie would like it there. One day real soon she'd slip in and look around again.

All she needed was a hidey-hole for herself and Billie. And a way to get food.

She lifted the top layer of rags off the cart. By the candle's uncertain light, his flushed little face looked up at her. Now he stretched and blinked and yawned.

Still sleepy, the little lamb! Snug in his blanket and lulled by the movement of the cart and the sweet, strong cough syrup, he'd slept all day.

He began to whimper.

"Hush, hush." She picked him up out of the cart and stroked his small hot forehead. Tears blurred her eyes. Billie, Billie, her heart sang. The Lord has given you back to me. I found you under a bush, curled up with your blanket like a baby rabbit, fast asleep. I picked you up in my arms and tucked you into my cart and covered you up, and you never even stirred!

He was awake now. He began to cry, a high thin wail.

"Stop that now, Billie!"

He put his thumb in his mouth and made convulsive, sucking movements with his swollen little mouth. Pooh! how he smelled! She should have changed him yesterday. She'd always hated to change his diapers. They'd told her that other time that she should have changed him oftener and kept him clean.

She unwrapped him from his blanket and pulled off the small, soaked jeans. Her gnarled fingers struggled with the tapes of his overflowing diaper. These newfangled diapers were strange. She rummaged in the cart and pulled out a filthy, torn T-shirt. She dropped the soiled diaper to the floor.

When he was as clean as she could get him, she folded the T-shirt into the semblance of a diaper and awkwardly put it around him. She shoved his rubbery little legs back into his jeans and wrapped him up again in his blanket.

She left him on the bed while she dug in the cart for the whisky. She poured some into a cracked glass and added a few drops of water from the plastic jug she kept filled from a leaking hydrant on the street.

When she turned around again, he had loosened the blanket, scrambled to the edge of the bed and was sliding off it. She held out the glass. "Want something good, Billie?"

He backed away from her. There was fear in his face. But when she continued to hold out the glass, he looked at it and slowly started toward it. When he was close enough, she put down the glass and grabbed him.

She sat down on the bed with Billie on her lap and held the glass to his lips. He opened his mouth and took a greedy swallow. Then he gulped and spat and began to cry. His legs stiffened and he kicked wildly.

"Bad boy, Billie!" She put the glass down again and gave Billie a smart slap across the face. Her hand left a welt on his cheek. He gasped and looked at her with terror. Then he screwed up his face and shrieked.

"Billie! Haven't you learned yet? You must not yell!"

Footsteps.

She clamped her hand over Billie's mouth. They were here! They'd come to take him away!

"Watcha screechin' for, Lou? Sounds like you bein' killed in here."

Gus. She went limp with relief, but she kept her hand over Billie's mouth and with her other hand she tried to control his thrashing arms and legs. "Mind your own business, you old fart!" she called to Gus. "I ain't screechin'. It's them fucking cats down there. You're too deaf to know the difference. Bug off!"

She heard him mumble something obscene as he shuffled away and up the stairs to his own stinking hole.

She took her hand away from Billie's mouth. He gasped and took a long, dragging breath. Then he squeezed his eyes shut and squared his mouth. He was going to yell. She had to make him learn he could not do that.

When the lesson was over, Billie lay limp and still. She took a long swallow from the bottle. The whisky went down like fire, warming her all the way to her arthritic toes. She picked Billie up again and held him, rocking him back and forth. He was soft and snuggly, the way she wanted him to be, and quiet except for a shudder now and then that shook his little frame.

He was her baby. This time she would take care of him. Tomorrow she'd take the money that light-haired man had dropped on the sidewalk and she'd go over to Broadway and buy Billie some milk.

She had her baby back again. They'd taken him away in the ambulance when the bad time began, and they told her she was too young and too stupid to take care of him right. The fucking bitch who roomed next door told the cops she starved her baby and beat him.

It wasn't true. She'd fed him when she had money to buy food. As for beating him—couldn't they understand how that crying got on her nerves? She was only trying to teach him not to cry so much.

Before they took him away they pointed to the scars on his face and the bruises on his legs and his little bottom raw and bleeding and they told her she wasn't fit to take care of him.

They said she'd abused him. He was starving, they said, and it was her fault. And they said she'd almost killed him by giving him so many aspirins.

After they took him away, they took her away too, and put her in a room that had bars at the window. A couple of days later they told her he was dead.

That's when she went crazy. That was the bad time. She didn't know how long she was in that place and then another place, but finally one day they let her out. It must've been a hospital, not a jail, because it was a doctor who told her she was OK now and she could take care of herself. They were letting her go.

She came back to New York on a bus. It was the only place she wanted to be. She'd learned how to take care of herself. A hand-out here, a free meal there, a grating or a doorway to sleep in when they threw her out of Grand Central and Port Authority. She'd gotten tougher and craftier and she'd lasted a long time.

After a while she knew why she'd lasted so long. Billie was coming back to her. She was going to find him again.

The Lord told her that. She'd never had much to do with the Lord personally in spite of her folks dragging her to church all the time when she was a kid. But one day she'd wandered into the cathedral to get out of the rain and she heard the organ and the singing and then she heard the preacher talking about the shepherd who went out to look for the little lost lamb and found him, and she knew it was the Lord's voice telling her to look for Billie.

That's when she began her search. Summers were the best time. Children swarmed on the playgrounds in the park. People brought babies in strollers and carriages. At first she would go right up to them and peer at the little faces, but when she found that the mothers were frightened of her, she stopped doing that. She didn't want them to call the cops and have her put away again. After that she just hung around the playgrounds and watched from a distance. She knew one day she would find Billie.

And here he was, warm in her arms! Another big swallow of whiskey made her feel like singing. She was full of glory like she was in the cathedral when the organ boomed out and engulfed her in sound. Billie would like to hear that. Billie would like to live in the cathedral. They'd be safe there, dry and—well, not really warm. Those old stones were cold as winter itself. But they'd be inside, out of the rain and snow. She'd keep Billie wrapped tight in his blanket. She'd find a place for them.

"Praise the Lord!" she sang. "Billie, praise the Lord!"

She shook him, but he did not praise the Lord. The candle was guttering, so low in the saucer now that its light was almost out. She couldn't see Billie's face. He was breathing raggedly through his mouth.

"Good boy, Billie," she murmured. His little body was limp, and he was growing warmer and warmer as she held him and rocked him and sang praises to the Lord.

TWENTY-ONE

ROBERT LAWRENCE ORSINE stood in line at the Red Apple Supermarket at noon on Saturday and watched the checkout clerk bag groceries for the woman ahead of him.

He knew who she was. He was sure no one else in the store did. Yesterday after work and this morning he'd hung around on the fringe of the crowd still bunched in front of the Fosters' building. He'd looked carefully at everyone who went in and out. It hadn't taken him long to memorize the faces of the people who lived in the building. A young Oriental couple were in the back apartment. Two women lived in the front. The top two floors were the Fosters'.

The short, monkey-faced man was the detective, García, the one who made statements for the papers—"Police continue to follow up clues in the sex slaying of baby-sitter Lorna Meyers, Detective García of the Central Park Precinct said today."

What crap!

An older couple had arrived by cab and been escorted inside by the cops. A set of parents? A heavy woman went in and came out again yesterday. Could be a cleaning lady. And there was a bunch of cops.

At first he hadn't paid much attention to the skinny woman in the sunglasses and scarf. He'd seen her leave and come back a couple of times, and he'd picked her for one of the women in the front apartment. Then he looked again. She resembled the woman he'd seen yesterday, but she didn't walk the same. Her stride was longer, and her body was more exciting to watch.

He followed her over to Broadway. When the big beefy guy who was obviously a plainclothes cop fell in behind her, he was sure. In the supermarket she'd whisked off the glasses to take a quick look at the label on a cereal box. He saw her face.

Pat Foster was grocery shopping. She must have gotten tired of waiting in her apartment for the phone call that never came.

She'd put on a scarf and glasses like the woman's downstairs, and she'd walked out her front door bold as brass.

He looked at every item the checkout clerk rang up for her. Coffee, two big cans. Five loaves of bread, assorted kinds—rye, whole wheat, pumpernickel. A big order of cold cuts and cheese from the deli counter. Looked like they were making sandwiches for that army of cops staked out in their apartment.

Soap. Toilet paper. A roast beef. Frozen vegetables. Potatoes. Cereal. Lettuce and tomatoes. Two cartons of half-and-half—that was to go with the coffee. And a five-pound bag of sugar.

When the last item was bagged and Pat Foster handed over the money, Orsine almost laughed out loud.

No milk!

He didn't know a hell of a lot about kids, but he did know one thing. They drank milk. Lots of it. Pat Foster hadn't bought so much as one fucking quart.

The cop carried two bags of groceries. She carried the third one herself. He didn't have to follow her back to her apartment. He'd found out all he needed to know.

He paid for his own purchases, a box of crackers, a package of cheese, and a can of cold soda. Through the supermarket window he could see Pat and her escort climb into a cab. He knew all about the cabs that cruised up and down Broadway, never picking anybody up. The drivers were plainclothes cops.

He tucked his bag under his arm and walked slowly up Broadway. He'd cross over to the park by a different street. No use taking a chance that some smart-ass cop would remember him and wonder why he was walking past the Fosters' building so often.

In the park he sat on a bench and crunched the crackers, liking the snap of them between his teeth and the contrast with the smooth, bland cheese. He drank the soda in small swallows, savoring it. The weather was cool, but so clear and bright he was glad he had his snazzy tinted glasses.

The park didn't seem like the same place it was on Monday when it was wet and gray and cold. He scowled. His muddy running shoes were still in the back of his closet. He'd have to get rid of them like he'd gotten rid of the jogging suit.

Excitement raced through him suddenly. Saving himself was now a challenge as demanding as stalking Lorna. This time the stakes were higher. That dark, rainy Monday when he looked down at Lorna's body and her bulging, accusing eyes, he thought he'd destroyed his reason for living.

Since then he'd had one stroke of luck after another.

And now he was certain. Ricky Foster was still missing.

The blacks. They were the ones. They were so afraid the cops would try to pin rape and murder on them that they'd grabbed the kid and done away with him. They'd panicked and run, but later they'd come back and made sure there was no witness.

They'd done what he would've done if he hadn't lost his cool. They'd done it for him. Ricky was eliminated. The fact that his body wasn't found yet didn't mean a thing. He'd thought of a dozen places to hide a body that small.

He could stop worrying about Ricky. Whoever had given the description to the cops, it wasn't him.

Who was it?

That artist's drawing—he'd thought it was the way the kid had seen him. Now he knew better.

The old sucker in the wheelchair. He'd squinted at him with faded, nearsighted eyes. All he'd seen was hair and beard and glasses.

It had to be him. He'd be easy to find.

TWENTY-TWO

AT THE PLAYGROUND where Ricky and Lorna had spent so many hours, Mike met Robin and Jeanette Ruiz. Robin had bright black eyes and a head of frizzy dark hair. She straddled Mike's foot. "Horsey-ride!" she demanded.

"Get off Mister Marlowe's foot, Robin. He doesn't want to be a horse."

"I don't mind," Mike said hastily. He swung his foot up and down while the little girl clung to his leg and giggled.

"Enough, Robin!" said her mother. "Go play in the sandbox."

"You build a big castle and I'll come and look at it when it's finished," Mike smiled.

Robin slid off his foot. When she had seated herself in the sandbox and begun to dig earnestly with a large kitchen spoon, her mother turned to Mike. "When you called and asked if you could talk to me, Mr. Marlowe, I told you I didn't think I could be of much help. I told the cops everything I could remember about Lorna and Ricky, and believe me, it isn't much. We talked a little and the children played together. That's really all."

"You saw her the day she was killed?"

"Early in the afternoon, until about three. Then they left because they were going to meet someone who was waiting for them."

"Did she tell you anything about him?"

"No, but when she wanted to get Ricky out of the sandbox, she told him 'Mister Boo' would be looking for him, and Ricky came right away."

"You told the police that?"

"It was practically the first thing I told them."

"Did you see Lorna or Ricky after that?"

"No. When the rain started, I grabbed Robin and ran. Later when I turned on the news and heard about a dead woman and a missing child, I said 'Oh, my God, that sounds like Lorna and Ricky!' I called the police. García and another detective came over to ask me the same questions you're asking me now."

"Did Lorna ever say anything, hint anything, about meeting anyone in the park other than this Mister Boo?"

"The answer is no. And, like I told García, Lorna was quiet. Didn't talk much about personal things. We mostly watched the children play."

"Did you ever see her with a man?"

"I did not! You're not one of those, are you Mr. Marlowe?"

"One of what?"

"One of those men who thinks if a girl gets raped she had to have let some man think she wanted it? If that's what you think, this interview is over!" She was poised to snatch Robin out of the sandbox and run.

He held out his hand, touched her arm. "You've got to believe me, I'm as angry as you are that this terrible thing happened to Lorna Meyers. I feel guilt and shame as well when another man does this. I want to find him. And if this Mister Boo isn't the man, and for some reason García is sure he isn't, there's a man out there somewhere."

She set back. "OK. I get it. But the answer is still no. I have no idea if there was a man. The only thing I can remember her saying about herself was that she was tired."

"When was that?"

"A couple of weeks ago. She looked dragged out, and I asked her what was the matter. She said she was working real hard at school, had a paper due, the first one in a course, and she'd been up late writing it. She said that when she finally got to sleep, she had a bad dream, like a nightmare. It woke her up, and she didn't get back to sleep after that."

A nightmare. Mike's senses came alert. "Did she tell you what the nightmare was about?"

"No, but she said something funny about it—"

Mike was conscious of tension. In his mind something stirred.

Jeanette went on, "She said something like 'it was a dream I used to have, but I haven't dreamed it in a long time.'"

"Did you tell García that Lorna had a nightmare?"

"I didn't think of it at the time. My God—do you think it was a premonition?"

"Not exactly. It could be of no importance." Mike was silent. This unexpected fact connected with Lorna Meyers was giving rise to an idea so farfetched and yet so logical that it made the hairs stand up on the back of his neck.

He was glad that Jeanette changed the subject. "García showed me the picture. I never saw anyone who looked like that anywhere near Ricky or Lorna."

"You know more about children than I do. Is there a chance that Ricky might have wandered back here after Lorna was killed? Looking for you and Robin?"

"I doubt it. And if he did, poor little fellow, Robin and I were gone by that time."

"When you were leaving the park, did you see any strangers wheeling carriages or strollers? Anyone with a child wrapped up so his face was hidden?"

"García asked me the same questions and got the same answer—No. I saw no mysterious strangers. No one carrying a kid the way you describe. I know all the kids who play here and who brings them. We all left at the same time except for the ones who were smart enough to start home before the rain."

He was desperate now. "Did you see anyone carrying a suitcase, or maybe a big, heavy duffel bag?"

"My God!" Her eyes went to the little girl playing in the sandbox. "Is that how he got Ricky out of the park? The kid would have to have been dead—or unconscious. No healthy two-year-old would allow himself to be stuffed into a suitcase."

"Maybe he was drugged. It's a thought."

"It's a lousy thought."

"I've run out of good ones."

"Remember, Mr. Marlowe, it was raining really hard. I wasn't paying attention to anything but getting Robin and myself home. Just because I didn't see a man run out of the park with Ricky doesn't mean it didn't happen."

"It's almost unbelievable that someone didn't see him."

"Do you know if García talked to the bag lady? She's always hanging around this part of the park. She watches the kids. She might have seen something."

"The bag lady? You mean that old woman with the cart? I saw her yesterday."

"Of course the cops would have a hard time getting anything sensible out of her. She's a religious nut."

"García said they questioned drunks and derelicts, so I assume they questioned her. Have you seen her today?"

"No, I haven't. She must have a hiding place nearby—one of those empty buildings on Cathedral or Amsterdam. It must be getting pretty cold there at night. Maybe she's moved downtown to a warm grating."

"Come see my castle?" Robin piped.

Mike admired the mounds of sand studded with twigs and stones. He rewarded the builder with another horsey-ride.

"Good luck, Mr. Marlowe," said Jeanette. "I'm sorry I wasn't more help."

"Maybe you were more help than you know. Or than I know at this point. Thank you."

He was forming a theory as tenuous as the nightmare on which it was based.

Julie had nightmares. Three years later, in the quiet, expensive haven they'd had to put her in, she still had them. Night after night she had screamed, and his mother had gone in to rock and murmur and try to comfort the hurt, terrified child Julie had become.

His father was grieved—and helpless. Mike, too. Julie wouldn't let any man, not even her father or her brother, get close enough to touch her.

He had to look into Lorna's past. That was going to bring him, sooner or later, face to face again with Linda.

TWENTY-THREE

GILBERT ORTIZ laughed out loud as his sneakers hit the pavement. Slap! Slap! Man, he felt good! Looked good, too, a cool dude in a neat blue running suit. The pants were light and loose, the sweatshirt a little too big, but what the hell? He felt great as he loped along the park's West Drive.

He'd been lucky Monday night when he was hurrying home from work. The color had caught his eye, that bright blue wadded up in the trash basket. He'd almost missed it as he ran head down against the rain across the park from Mt. Sinai.

Quickly as he could, he'd pulled it out. First the pants, then the shirt. He'd put them into the gym bag he carried his white uniform in.

Some dude sure was crazy to throw away a perfectly good running suit. Had the mother gone home naked? Nothing wrong with it that Gilbert could see except for a brownish stain down the side of one pant leg.

Slap! Slap! Gilbert began to puff. Sweat ran down his face and into his beard. He was outta shape, no doubt about that. If he was gonna run like these tall, straining white men who were warming up for the marathon tomorrow, he'd have to get in better shape. They caught up with him and passed him so easily.

"You! Stop! Police officer!"

Gilbert looked around. A cop was pounding behind him, gun at the ready. Jesus! Who was he after? Ahead of him the other runners were looking back too. He could see their white, frightened faces. They began to scatter in all directions. Cyclists as well as runners careened wildly off onto the grass.

"You in the blue suit! Freeze!"

Sirens. A cop car squealing down the drive. Another one. More guns.

Holy shit, it was *him* they were after!

They were on him. Gilbert began to scream. "Man, I ain't done nothin'!" Then he took refuge in his mother tongue. "No comprendo" was all they got out of him for a very long time.

TWENTY-FOUR

TODAY WAS THE LAST TIME. Tomorrow the park would be mobbed with people coming to watch the marathon runners on their last leg—down Fifth Avenue, into the park at 102nd, and on down the drive to the finish, three miles farther on.

Crowds pushing and jostling. No place for an old man in a wheelchair.

A tired, grieving old man. He'd go to the park today and sit where he always waited for Ricky and Lorna. He would be alone. It would be his farewell to the young woman and the little boy who had so briefly brightened his life.

And who had been so cruelly taken. He had no hope that Ricky, missing since Monday, could still be alive. The world was cruel and violent and cold. Winter was closing in. He did not want to live for another spring.

Detective García had told him to stay in his apartment for a few days in case the man in the blue suit came back looking for the witness who had given them the description. But he no longer believed in the man in the blue suit.

He was sure that García didn't either.

It had been coincidence, no more. The man who sat down on the bench across from them was just a jogger stopping to rest. Bad eyesight and an overworked imagination had made him see the man's eyes on Lorna behind those dark glasses.

The police had been skeptical from the start. And there'd been no sign of the man since. No clue in Lorna's death. And no trace of Ricky.

He drew his chair close to the benches under his favorite tree with the branches spread low over the place where Lorna had sat. The little boy played on the sidewalk at their feet, or climbed into his lap, his warm, wiggly little body electric with excitement when he'd given him a ride.

Loneliness had vanished. He'd been happy then—loved and wanted.

The too-easy tears of old age were spilling now, wetting his furrowed cheeks. He'd sat right there that day and watched them hurry away to get home before the rain. His fault. He'd kept them too long, delaying them by insisting that Ricky have one more ride, even after he'd seen Lorna's nervous glance at the sky. If he had let them go sooner, they wouldn't have been alone when the man—

"Are you OK, Pop?" The husky voice came from a man leaning over him.

He fumbled for a handkerchief, ashamed that a stranger had caught him weeping. "I'm all right," he said gruffly. "Caught a chill. Bad cold." He wiped his eyes.

The stranger sat down on the bench, right where Lorna had sat. The lightly tinted glasses he was wearing did not hide the concern in his dark eyes. He was a big man, heavily muscular. Like most young people these days, he was wearing jeans, with a light windbreaker over a sweater. "I'm not leaving you until I'm sure you're all right," he said with pleasant firmness.

Harold Bloor blew his nose and gave his face a final swipe. "I was remembering a lovely young woman who used to sit with me here. She's dead now."

"That's tough, Pop. Was she a relation of yours?"

"No, just a park acquaintance. But she was kind to an old man. She listened to me so patiently when I rambled on. And the little boy she was taking care of was such a bright little fellow."

The man gave a low whistle. "Jesus, Pop! You're not talking about that girl who was killed here Monday? And the kid that was snatched? No wonder you felt like crying!"

Harold Bloor bristled. He hated to be called Pop. He was sorry now he'd confided so much in this stranger. He wanted the man to go away and leave him to his grief.

He seemed to have no intention of doing so. He stretched out his legs comfortably and went on chattily, "I suppose the police questioned you about her?"

"Oh, yes. I was one of the last people to see her alive."

"No kidding!"

The old man's irritation eased. It was good to talk to someone. He'd held it in too long. The police were interested only in facts. They'd been impatient with his slow memory. They hadn't cared how he felt.

"Yes, indeed. I called the police the next day when I read in the paper what happened to Lorna. I thought I could help them find the man who did it."

"Really? How come?"

"I'd seen a man I thought was staring at her. He sat over there and she was right where you are. You must have read about him in the papers. He was wearing a blue running suit."

"You gave that description to the cops? Wow, Pop! That was good of you. To come forward, I mean. Most people don't want to get involved. They're scared of cops, scared of being a witness. Or they just don't want to bother."

"It was the only thing I could do. The girl had been kind to me. I wanted to help the police find her killer. I'm afraid I was of very little use, though."

"What makes you think that?"

The man's interest was positively flattering now. Harold Bloor felt himself come alive. "I think I just imagined that man was staring at Lorna. My eyes aren't too good anymore."

"Think you'd recognize him if you saw him again?"

Harold Bloor gave a bitter chuckle. "Hard to say. But if there is such a man and he reads the paper, surely he's shaved off his beard and cut his hair by this time!"

"How about the kid? Did he see the guy? Would he be likely to remember him?"

"Ricky's a very bright little boy for two."

"Pretty smart, is he? Talks real plain?"

"Oh, yes! One minute he's a real little man, climbing out of the stroller and running to meet me. 'Gimme a wide, Mister Boo!' he'd say. Then a little while later he's almost a baby again, the way he was the last time I saw him. Lorna had put him in the stroller to take him home. He was rubbing his eyes, about to fall asleep, and he had his blanket around him—"

"What's the matter, Pop?"

Harold Bloor did not answer. Something tugged at him. Some wisp of memory he could not get hold of. He'd blanked from his mind everything that had happened since Tuesday when he'd come to the park with his newspaper and opened it to find that Lorna and Ricky would never come to meet him again.

He'd gone back to his apartment and sat, sick and frozen with grief. Finally he'd roused himself to call the police. They'd come, asked him questions until he was exhausted, warned him not to go out and not to talk to anyone. He'd spent the intervening days numbed. It was Harriet's death all over again. Such a waste of young lives!

Now he struggled to bring memory back. Somewhere in those lost days he had seen something. Something important.

The friendly stranger was on his feet. "Hey, Pop, you don't look too good. Can I take you home? Take you someplace to get a drink, cup of coffee?"

"Hush!" Bloor spoke crossly. He wanted this chattering fool to be quiet so he could remember. He tried to see the park the way it was on Tuesday when he'd wheeled himself to the spot where he would wait.

"Pop?"

"What was I talking about?"

"When, Pop?" the man sounded alarmed.

"Just now. I was talking about Ricky. What did I say?"

His new friend sat down again, but poised on the edge of the bench. "You were telling me about him falling asleep in the stroller the last time you saw him."

"The blanket!"

"What blanket? The kid's blanket, you mean?"

"It wasn't blue! It was gray because it had been washed so often. Lorna told me that they had to sneak it away from him while he was asleep, run it through the washer and dryer and put it back before he woke up and missed it. Poor little boy, how lost he must be without it!"

"What are you talking about, Pop? They found the stroller and the toy truck, but they didn't find no blanket. Whoever took the kid took him blanket and all."

"He dropped it. That must be what happened. She found it someplace and picked it up. She collects rags. Her cart is full of them."

"Who picked it up? Who's 'she'?"

His mind had raced ahead of his ability to make his mouth form the words. He had to make sense. He had to make this man understand, get him to help. "The old woman!" He got it out at last. "The old woman with the shopping cart! The police will make her tell them where she found Ricky's blanket. We've got to get to the police!" Blood was singing in his ears, and, chilly as it was, he had begun to sweat. He groped for the switch. He had to get home to phone Detective García.

The man jumped up. His eyes blazed behind the glasses. "Take it easy, Pop. One step at a time. You say you saw the kid's blanket somewhere *after* he disappeared?"

"That's what I'm trying to tell you! It's that old woman, the bag lady. Ricky's blanket was in her shopping cart, stuffed in with all the rest of her rags. I saw it, but I was so shocked by reading about Lorna and Ricky that I didn't remember it. I didn't remember anything about that day until just now when I was talking to you."

"OK, old fellow." The man was bending over him. "Just tell me once more, slow and easylike, where and when you saw this blanket."

"The day after Lorna . . . died. Tuesday. The old woman passed me with her cart. Just over there. It's a clue, don't you see? If the police can get her to tell them where she found the blanket, they might find—" The meaning of what he was saying got through to him. An ominous numbness spread through his left arm. He groped again for the switch.

The stranger's hands were on his shoulders. "OK, Pop, I got the picture now. Would you like me to call the cops? I'll tell them you think you saw the kid's blanket in the bag lady's cart the day after he disappeared."

Harold Bloor slumped with relief. "Yes, please. Tell them."

"I'll go find a phone. Then I'll come back and report. The cops will want to talk to you. Will you wait here?"

"No, I think I'd better go back to my apartment. I don't feel so well. García knows where I live. I'll wait for him there."

"Tell me where you live. I'll come to your place as soon as I've called the cops. There's a pay phone around here someplace."

"I'm not far—between Fifth and Madison." He gave the man his address and added, "My name is Harold Bloor. What's yours?"

"You can call me Bob." He was smiling now. His teeth were strangely small and pearly for so large a man. "Do you know where this old lady hangs out? The cops will want to know where they can find her."

"I have no idea where that poor creature finds shelter. Somewhere on the west side of the park, perhaps. I've never seen her on Fifth Avenue. I hope when the police find her, they can get her to make sense. She's quite demented, I'm afraid."

"You go on back to your apartment and sit tight, Mr. Bloor. I'll check back with you as soon as I can. Wait for me, OK? And just to play safe, don't say anything to anyone about what you and me discussed. I mean, we don't want to screw things up for the cops, do we?"

Harold Bloor made his slow way out of the park. The numbness in his arm had turned into a dull ache. He was sad and exhausted, but relieved. Whatever happened, he had finally been able to do something that might help the police find Ricky.

TWENTY-FIVE

"OK, LET'S HAVE that again," said García patiently.

Gilbert Ortiz, wrapped in a blanket, was sweating. One cop had been sent to Harold Bloor's apartment to bring in the old man to look at a lineup. Another was on his way to Gilbert's room to bring him some clothes.

Gilbert had waived his right to counsel. He was already sorry he had done so. "Estoy—" he began.

"Speak English!"

"OK, OK, like I said, Monday evenin' it's rainin' hard an' I'm on my way home from work—from Mt. Sinai, I'm an orderly there. I spots this blue in the trash an' I pulls it out and puts it in my bag. Today I puts it on an' come over here to run. I'm runnin', mindin' my own business. Next thing happen is the fuckin' cops is all over me. Don't see you pullin' in any white dudes. Why me? You ain't told me nothin'. I got my rights!"

"Did you see the man who threw away the suit?"

"Didn't see no one. But he sure is one dumb shit to throw out a suit good as that. You gonna give it back to me?"

"Did anyone see you pull the suit out of the trash?"

"Dunno. Don't think so."

"Where is the trashbasket?"

"I already tell you that, man. Chained to a post. Near 96th."

"Have you read the papers or watched TV this week?"

"TV. Some. Why you askin'?"

"A woman was raped and killed in the park Monday evening."

"Yeah, I seen that. What's it got to do with me?"

"She was seen earlier with a man. He was wearing a suit like that. His hair and beard were like yours."

"Hey, man, I don't know nothin' about that! You shoulda told me. I wanna lawyer!"

"The killer may be the man who threw away the suit."

The unbearded portions of Gilbert's olive face paled to a dirty yellow. "I been wearin' murderer's clothes? Shit, man!"

"Did you wash the suit before you put it on?"

"Why should I? It wasn't dirty."

"Put out your hands—OK, now palms up."

There were no half-healed bite wounds on Ortiz's hands. García's jaw muscles relaxed slightly. All his instincts told him that Ortiz was not the man, but with luck the suit could be the first break. The lab might find hairs—other than Ortiz's—semen, blood that matched the girl's. And if the stain on the left leg had come from a man wiping a bleeding hand...

Excitement buoyed him suddenly. He'd too quickly dismissed Harold Bloor's story. The ephemeral "man in blue" was becoming a human being, a body that had filled that suit and left its telltale evidence. This time he would listen carefully to the old man.

"OK, Ortiz. When your clothes come, you get dressed. I've got someone coming to take a look at you."

Why was it taking so long for them to bring Harold Bloor in?

TWENTY-SIX

HE MUST NOT RUN. Act normal. He was a man out taking a little stroll.

Orsine forced his feet to move, one in front of the other. He pushed away waves of panic that made him want to look back over his shoulder, stare wildly up and down the street. His whole body was wet with sweat. He wanted to vomit.

Easy. Slow. Hadn't he learned from what happened after Lorna—?

If you don't panic, you've got it made. Keep cool. Don't blow this one, Orsine. Keep your mind on going into the park and across it to somewhere on the West Side where you're going to track down that crazy old bitch who's been trundling Ricky Foster around in a shopping cart ever since Monday.

The old man's wild idea about the kid's blanket made everything fall into place. That noise he'd heard after the niggers took off—it must've been her.

Don't think about what you left behind this time, Orsine. Don't wonder if someone saw you come out of the old man's building. Or go into it. Roll up the windbreaker and throw it into the first trash you come to. Chuck the old man's wallet into the next one. Pretty smart move, taking that wallet. Let the cops think the old man surprised a burglar and keeled over from fright.

Orsine's stomach heaved. So fucking easy.

He'd waited until he was sure Bloor had had time to get home. Then he'd followed him. He wasn't going to take a chance this time by leaving a witness alive, no matter what the guy had said about not being able to recognize the man in blue without his beard.

He hadn't even had to lay a hand on him. Just told him the truth. Laughed in his face and watched him fall out of the chair.

Dead when he hit the floor.

He'd run around then and wiped everything he could remember he'd touched. He'd been so excited he had to pee. He'd remembered to wipe the john handle. Then he'd taken the wallet from the old man's pocket. He'd put his handkerchief over his hand when he let himself out the door.

No one had stopped him.

Too easy? Was his luck going to run out?

The handkerchief reminded him. Ricky. Ricky would remember the bandanna wabbit. And the man who had made it. He was going to get that kid. For sure. Then there wouldn't be anyone left who could connect him with Lorna. He'd be safe. He could start forgetting.

He was trembling when he reached the corner of Fifth Avenue. The sidewalk was crowded. People were coming home from work. He had to skirt around two prancing Dobermans and their owner. He must not draw attention, human or canine, by darting across the street. He had to wait for the light. Be cool and calm. He'd learned.

He hadn't killed the old man. He had to remember that and not act like he was guilty or afraid. If his luck held, he might not have to kill Ricky either. Five days in the hands of that mad old bitch couldn't have done the kid any good. Maybe he was dead already.

Sirens! Oh, Jesus. Someone had seen him!

A cop car careened down Fifth Avenue. When it came to the corner, it slewed around it and raced by him. Halfway down the block it pulled up in front of Harold Bloor's apartment.

When he saw the cops get out, Orsine lost his cool. He began to run.

TWENTY-SEVEN

MIKE LEFT Jeanette and Robin Ruiz and looked for a pay phone. He'd agreed to keep García informed. What would the detective think of his hunch? Probably not much. He might even laugh. But the clue suggested by Lorna's nightmare, vague as it was, might take García's mind off Edwin and Kent. Might make him look at the case from a different stance.

García, when he reached him, seemed almost affable. "Interesting that you should call just now," he said. "We've found a blue running suit. Apparently it was stuffed into a trash can in the park Monday evening. Picked up by a guy who wore it out running today."

"So now you're going back to all the people you questioned before and ask if they saw a guy running from the park in his jock?"

García laughed. "Shorts and a T-shirt underneath. That's streetwear these days. We already know the answer—no one saw a man, clothed or nude, with Ricky Foster. No cold, wet, half-dressed runners carrying a child on the subway or the bus."

"Which means that he walked—or ran—home."

"Or got into a vehicle on Central Park West. What's on your mind, Marlowe?"

"Lorna Meyers had nightmares."

"What's that supposed to mean?"

Mike's own words gave him a sinking feeling. This was too far-out to be plausible. Just as he expected, García laughed. "I think fiction is more your line than journalism, Marlowe. Why the hell are you bothering me with this?"

"Don't you see what it could mean? Lorna sees a man. The sight of him triggers something, makes her subconscious act up."

"Forget it! Give me facts, Marlowe, not psychological crap. I'll put my faith in the lab. Blood, semen, hair—"

"From a man who knew Lorna Meyers. Who stalked her."

"The stalking part I'll go along with. Few years ago we had a series of rapes in Riverside Park. Guy came out early in the morning in running gear and raped women joggers who were out there in shorts and T-shirts and not much on underneath. One got away and ran to the cops. We staked out the park with a female officer, and we got him. We'll get this guy. And eventually they'll get the guy who did it to your sister."

"What about Ricky?" Anger made him speak more sharply than he intended.

"I've got a call on another line. Goodbye, Marlowe. Don't waste any more of my time with dreams."

Mike hung up. That was that. He'd tried. García had brushed him off. What did he have to lose by going to Queens to pursue his hunch? Linda was already alienated; he could do her no more harm.

Lorna had nightmares. And an unexplained contradiction in her personality. In spite of the denials of family and friends, had there been a man in her life?

Quiet, serious, nunlike. Everyone who described her used those terms.

All but one.

On the train he planned his approach. He would say that he was doing an in-depth profile of Lorna Meyers, a magazine article that would attempt to resolve the contradictions of her life and death.

When he called Gertrude Simonson, Lorna's high school guidance counselor, she hesitated only briefly. Then she invited him to meet her in her office at the school where she was catching up on paperwork.

"I told the police what I know, Mister Marlowe. Frankly I'm curious about what you expect to get from this interview. That's why I agreed to see you. Lorna was a quiet girl and an honor student."

"As her counselor, how frequently did you see her?"

"Every spring we met to plan her courses. I try to see all my students two or three times a year, but with a counseling load as large as we have—"

"So you actually talked with her only a few times."

"I'm sorry to say that's true. If she'd been a problem student, I'd have seen her more often. As it was, our conferences were brief. She always knew what courses she needed and what electives she wanted."

"Are many of your students like her?"

Gertrude laughed. "If all my counselees were like Lorna Meyers, the guidance department could close its doors!"

"Did it ever occur to you that there was something unnatural in Lorna's goodness?"

"What do you mean?"

"That she was too quiet, too controlled?"

"As if she were concealing something?"

"Something like that."

She put her hands flat on the desk and pushed back as if she wanted to put more space between herself and Mike. "You want me to tell you things about Lorna that you can twist out of context and string together with insinuations so you can write another story that will further damage the reputation of a fine young woman? Good day, Mister Marlowe!"

"Mrs. Simonson, I didn't write the story you're referring to. I'm here because I want to be able to show my readers the real Lorna Meyers. My research into her personality could turn up something that would lead to the killer. Maybe he's a crazy man who was attracted to her *because* she was so quiet."

Gertrude compressed her lips. Mike felt that she wanted to believe him. "Did she ever come to you for personal counseling?" he asked.

"No, but I wish she had. This is one of the real tragedies of the public school. We don't have time to help so many who really need us."

"So you do think Lorna really needed help?"

"That degree of self-control in an adolescent is often a sign of deep-rooted problems. I knew from her records that she had lost both parents when she was twelve. Such losses can often evoke intense feelings of guilt. I did worry about her. I called her sister once to ask about Lorna's reticence.''

"What did Linda say?"

"She thanked me for my concern. That was all. Have you talked to Linda, Mister Marlowe?"

"Not since I interviewed her on Monday night. Did you tell the police any of this about Lorna's unnatural self-control?"

"I tried, but they weren't interested. They only wanted to know the names of boys who had shown an interest in Lorna. I told them there were none as far as I knew. They asked me about Pat Foster's contact with me and about my recommendation of Lorna as a sitter for their child."

"Did Lorna have many friends? Girl friends?"

"She and Kathy Rosen were close for a while. They were quite a contrast in personality, Lorna so quiet and Kathy so ebullient."

"Do you have Kathy Rosen's address?"

"Will I give it to you, don't you mean?"

He smiled. "Yes, that's what I mean."

"I talked with Kathy briefly at Linda's after the funeral. She's working as a cashier at Alexander's in the shopping center down a few blocks. She's in accessories—gloves, pocketbooks. Too bad she couldn't find a better job. She's really a bright young woman. Not a student like Lorna, of course, but capable."

Mike stood up. "I'm very grateful to you, Mrs. Simonson."

"I'm trusting you, Mr. Marlowe, you know that, don't you? I'm taking you at your word—you're going to write a story that will set the record straight on Lorna, undo the damage to her reputation of that insinuating 'Another Look.' "

"I hope to do more than that."

He found Kathy Rosen about to take her late afternoon supper break. He accompanied her to McDonald's in the mall, and while she ate a Big Mac and drank a milkshake, he questioned her.

Like everyone else he'd talked to, Kathy started by saying, "What can I tell you? I answered all the questions the cops asked. I'm really glad, though, that you're doing an article on

Lorna, and I can tell you the absolute truth—she had no boy-friends in high school.''

"I'm not so much interested in her relationships as I am in her personality. What words would you use to describe her?''

"Shy—quiet—sweet. Didn't talk a whole lot about herself. Like I said, no boyfriends, no fooling around. She didn't smoke or drink or take drugs.''

"How many years did you know her?''

"Since high school. We got to be friends in chemistry our junior year. She was real good in chem and I was a klutz at it. Mister Bondi put us together as lab partners. Best grade I ever got in science! I had a lot of respect for Lorna, believe me, Mr. Marlowe. I still can't believe it. It's so terrible!'' She put her sandwich back on the plate and wiped her eyes with her napkin.

"Please call me Mike.''

"OK, Mike.'' She recovered enough to take another bite of the Big Mac.

"What did other students think of her?''

"Too good to be true.''

"Did you think that?''

"Kind of, yes. Something about her wasn't quite—how can I say it? It was like there was a piece missing in her personality.''

"As if she were hiding something?''

"No, not like that. Lorna just didn't have any fun. She had no—spontaneity. When I found out both her parents had died the same year, I figured she'd been, you know, traumatized. She wasn't friendly until you got to know her. Boys fell all over her because of her looks, but she wouldn't give them the time of day, so they let her alone after that.''

"Did she ever say anything about men in her life?''

Kathy looked puzzled. "I just told you. Any boy who showed an interest, she turned him right off. I don't mean she was a lesbian. I mean, we were good friends, but she never made a pass at me.'' Then she got his meaning. "Oh! You mean *men*! You think that's why she didn't go for high school boys?''

"Is that a possibility?''

"I don't think so. Lorna didn't go for men either. I remember one day in chem lab, Mr. Bondi came over to see how we were doing with our experiment. He leaned over to look and put his arm around Lorna, kind of fatherlike. She fainted."

"Fainted? Right there in the lab?"

"Yep, she just got whiter and whiter and all of a sudden she was sliding off the lab stool and onto the floor. We brought her round with water, then I walked her down to the nurse's office. She was real embarrassed. Afraid everyone would think she was getting her period. She said the fumes from the experiment made her sick, but fumes had never bothered her before, and we burned some pretty rotten stuff. I've always thought she fainted because Mr. Bondi got too close. And he was OK, you know? Didn't smell or have bad breath like a lot of teachers."

"Did she ever say anything that explained why she didn't want Mr. Bondi to touch her? Or why she didn't like boys?"

"I asked her once, but she got real cool with me. Like I said, Lorna didn't talk a lot about herself."

"What did she say when you asked her that?"

"She said she had better things to do, something like that. You really oughta talk to Linda. I think it would be good for her to have someone to talk to besides cops and reporters. Oh! I forgot!"

"You're right. It's hard on Linda to have so many people asking nosy questions about her sister's private life."

Kathy had finished her meal. She was winding a striped scarf around her neck, preparing to go back to work. "The cops don't seem to be doing much. I mean, all I read is 'police continue to comb park for clues.' They don't have any leads, do they?"

"Police work is slow sometimes, Kathy. I know Detective García is working very hard on this investigation."

"It's weird, isn't it? Out there somewhere is a man who's getting away with rape and murder? Say, Mike, maybe you shouldn't write that stuff about Lorna fainting in the lab. It might embarrass Linda."

"I'll check with her before any of this gets into print. Thanks for your help, Kathy."

Linda. He was getting closer and closer to the moment when he would have to face Linda again.

In the end it was Linda who came to him.

TWENTY-EIGHT

THE DOOR to Lorna's room was still closed.

She brought a brown paper bag from the kitchen and went resolutely into the bathroom. She could not bring herself to open that bedroom door, but she would dispose of Lorna's toiletries, the reminder, every time she opened the cabinet, of the girl who would never use them again.

She could not bear to use them herself.

Into the bag Linda dropped Lorna's brush and comb, her shower cap, her shampoo. Her deodorant and toothbrush. A tube of colorless lip gloss.

There was little else. No mascara or eye shadow. No blusher. Lorna had denied her beauty and her femininity, and she'd used nothing that would enhance either.

She hadn't always been so austere. More than once, when she was growing up, she had helped herself to Linda's cosmetics. The last time was just before they found out Daddy was so sick. Linda remembered how furious she was to see her lipstick and mascara making Lorna look so much older than twelve. They'd quarreled.

Then—it could only have been a few days later—Mom told them Daddy was going to die. Lorna had changed from a boisterous pre-teen to a solemn young adult.

Too solemn. And she had changed too swiftly.

Linda closed her eyes. Was that double tragedy all that had snuffed out Lorna's vitality?

I should have—

She pushed down the thought. She ran cold water and splashed her face. Whatever she should have done to draw Lorna out of her sudden and precocious maturity, it was too late now.

She took a can of baby powder from the shelf. Then a bottle of tanning lotion. She almost smiled at this reminder of Lorna's one feminine vanity. She could not stand the sight of her pale legs when summer came and she wanted to go without panty hose. She'd bought the quick-tanning lotion and applied it every hour one June afternoon. She'd been pleased with the results. But the artificial tan had soon faded.

Absently, Linda opened the white plastic bottle. Its scent teased her. She'd smelled this recently. But where? Lorna hadn't used the stuff after that June day.

Someone had. Someone who had come close enough to her in the last few days that she had smelled it on his skin. There had been so many people this past week. Police. Reporters. Crowds of gawkers outside the building. The mourners who had been here after the funeral on Thursday. It could have been anyone in that mob.

The phone rang. Linda put the top back on the bottle of tanning lotion and threw it into the bag.

TWENTY-NINE

BILLIE DIDN'T WANT MILK. When she pushed the cup against his swollen lips, the milk ran out and dribbled down his neck. He stared at her with eyes that were glazed, fevered slits. He didn't cry anymore.

He was going to die.

She'd known since yesterday. She'd hoped the milk would make him better. That other time they'd told her she should have fed him milk.

Billie wouldn't drink it.

The Lord had given Billie back to her. Now the Lord was going to take him again. This time she wouldn't let the Lord send anyone else to get him. She'd take him to the Lord herself. She'd hide him where only the Lord could find him.

She didn't have a whole lot more time. If she didn't take him today, it would be too late. He'd die before she got him there.

Her fingers shook as she tried to hurry. She took off the wet jeans, and for the last time she made a diaper out of one of her rags. His little bottom was raw and sore like it was that other time. It was so hard to keep him clean. He smelled bad. His jeans were so filthy that she dropped them on the floor with the diaper and the other soiled rags. She wrapped him in his blanket. They didn't have far to go.

She dipped a corner of a rag into the plastic jug and wet it and dabbed at his face with it. She wanted the Lord to know that at least she'd tried to keep him clean. When she touched his lips and the welts on his cheeks, he flinched. A tiny, thin wail came out.

"No crying, Billie!"

His wail subsided into a soft moan. He put his thumb in his mouth and shut his eyes. She wrapped the blanket more securely around him. When she picked him up and put him into the cart, he made no protest. Good boy, Billie. Billie knew what was happening. His eyes opened once and he looked up at her dully. Then his head fell forward on his chest.

Asleep already. Good boy!

"We're going to for a ride, Billie boy, Billie boy," she sang. "We're going to the Lord, Billie boy, Billie boy. The Lord will take you in his arms. 'Suffer the little children to come unto me,' he said. I'm taking you to the Lord, Billie."

For a moment she stood motionless. She was going to lose him again. She'd been so happy these few days. Now the long empty years stretched before her again. Tears slid down the deep furrows of her face.

Lord, could you please take me, too?

She tucked a piece of an old brocade curtain around Billie and laid a folded bathmat on top of the cart. There was no movement within. Billie was ready for the journey to the Lord.

Getting out of the building was the hardest part. The cart was heavy with Billie in it. Down to the basement, push aside the door that was off its hinges. Go outside. Put the door back. Go up the stairs to the street level.

"Where ya goin', Lou?"

Gus. Stupid, drunken old Gus was braying at her as he staggered down the sidewalk. If she had something to hit him with she would kill him. People walking by were looking at them and laughing.

"Shut up you old fart!" she hissed in a loud whisper with as much menace as she could get in her voice. "You want the cops to know we live here?"

"Where ya goin'?" he repeated stubbornly. His red-rimmed eyes focused uncertainly.

"The Lord is waiting for me, I have to go." With dignity, she turned her back and pushed the cart to the corner. She looked across the street. She was in luck. A tour bus was just discharging a mob of chattering Japanese tourists slung about with cameras. They'd go inside in a bunch and mill around by the information desk. She'd be able to slip in unnoticed. She'd pull the cart to the top of the steps, then she'd take Billie out and carry him in her arms.

It would be risky, but she could do it. The Lord wanted her to bring Billie to him. He'd help her.

Once inside, she'd scurry down the side aisle and hide behind an altar in one of the chapels. When it was dark and everyone was gone, she'd creep out. She'd wander around that great cavern until she found the place.

She and Billie would wait there for the Lord.

THIRTY

"WHY ARE YOU asking questions about my sister?"

Coffee sloshed from Mike's cup. Intent on his notes, he had not seen Linda until she slipped into the booth and sat down across from him. She looked so much worse than she had on Monday—so much more grieved and stricken. Her face was thinner. Her eyes were dark with anger.

"How did you know?" He was caught, stupid as well as defenseless. The encounter had come too soon. Linda was sitting across from him, accusing him, and he was at a total loss.

"Gertrude called me the minute you left her office. I went to Alexander's to find Kathy. She told me she had just left you here. I don't know what you think you're doing, but I want you to stop! Haven't you done enough? To her? To me?"

He reached across the table. "Linda, please believe me. I'm trying to help you. I want to find the man who killed your sister."

She drew back. "Why? So you can win a Pulitzer Prize? So you can further destroy the reputation of a girl who never did anything to you? To anyone? Who's dead and can't defend herself? There are laws to protect people from snoops like you!"

"Listen to me. Give me one minute. That's all I ask."

"One minute." Her hands were gripping the purse in her lap so tightly that it shook.

He had to reach her. He had no time to be tactful. "I think the man who killed Lorna was someone she knew."

"No! Lorna didn't know any men. I told you that. Kathy told you the same thing. The police know that. Why can't you believe it? Can't you accept the fact that a girl can be normal and not be interested in men? Haven't you any decency?"

"I don't mean a man she was seeing recently. I mean way back—a long time ago."

For a second she was no longer angry. Her eyes were startled and naked. He couldn't guess the meaning of that look. Then she was out of the booth and running for the door.

He jumped up to follow. He looked up and down the sidewalk thronged with homegoing Saturday shoppers. Which way? He took a chance and went to the right.

He caught up with her in front of a shoe store. She was standing looking into the window as if she were intent on a display of boots. Her hands were over her face. She was shaking, either from crying or from the effort not to cry.

He spoke over her head to her reflection in the glass. "I'm asking questions because I want to know about her past. The police won't do that. García thinks he's getting closer to the killer, but he can't make an arrest until he has more evidence. By the time he gets it, it will be too late for Ricky Foster."

Her hands were still hiding her face, but she was no longer trembling. Something in her stillness told him she was listening. He thrust his handkerchief over her shoulder, touched her hand with it. When she looked to see what it was and then took it, he was electrified. Passersby were staring, but he ignored them. He spoke urgently to her bowed head. "If the police don't find him, he'll do it again. To another girl as lovely and innocent as your sister."

"This guy bothering you lady? Want me to call a cop?" Mike looked around and caught a gaze both hostile and curious from a plump man with a cigar in his mouth.

Linda turned around. "It's all right, he's not bothering me." She handed the handkerchief back to Mike. Her eyes were dry. "Mr. Marlowe," she said, "I think you and I should talk."

Mike felt a surge of surprising joy. By a miracle he had won her confidence. He knew he could make the most of it. "I have an idea," he said, "and please, Linda—call me Mike."

THIRTY-ONE

At LAST they were gone.

She had hidden in the ladies' room until the tourists had been herded back to their waiting bus. She had stayed in a toilet stall until she was sure the custodians had finished cleaning the cathedral for tomorrow. They swept and dusted and straightened the rows of chairs and made sure each kneeling cushion and prayer book was in place.

Now the custodians had gone, and there was no one in this vast, dark, vaulted space except her and Billie and the Lord.

She was where she wanted to be, on the long bench in the front row of the choir. The carved wood creaked under her weight. The olive-green velvet cushions smelled musty and old, but they were far softer than the sidewalk or the mattress in the room across the street. She hugged her coat about her tightly, for cold had begun to creep up from the stone floor.

Billie was safe. She'd found the perfect place. It had not been easy to put him there. She'd had to carry him such a long way. He was limp, wrapped in his blanket, and he was so heavy.

The Lord was here. He glowed on the great gold cross above the high altar. He glowed silently now, but he was gathering power. Soon he would blaze forth with glory and take her and Billie into his everlasting arms.

The Lord would know where to find them.

THIRTY-TWO

ORSINE CAME OUT of the park onto Central Park West. He looked up and down the avenue. Where had the old bitch gone? How many times had he seen her in the park when he was stalking Lorna, or wheeling her cart along Cathedral Parkway, or scrounging in the garbage by the markets on Broadway?

Now when he wanted her, she was no place in sight. She'd gone into some hiding place.

He had heard but not seen the ambulance that roared away with the earthly remains of Harold Bloor. An hour of walking in the park, of slow circling back to the West Side by an unhurried route, had persuaded him that no one was looking for him.

He'd gotten away with it. His luck had held once more. No one had seen him at Bloor's apartment. Now if he could find the old woman and her cart, he'd have it made. Follow her, get her alone—zap. Then Ricky.

He looked at his watch. Twenty minutes till five. The sky over the Hudson was aflame. If he didn't find her before dark, he'd have to wait until tomorrow.

He walked up Morningside. Would she hide somewhere around St. Luke's Hospital? Morningside Park? Not likely. Morningside Drive was a steep hill and that park was a rocky jungle.

She might have a hidey-hole somewhere in that warren of abandoned buildings in the blocks between Columbus and Amsterdam. He turned west and headed across 113th Street.

The huge, somber bulk of St. John the Divine loomed over him. Too many places there for her to hide in the gardens and grounds. If he didn't find her tonight, the cathedral grounds would be the first place he'd look tomorrow.

He looked up and down Amsterdam. No mumbling old woman crouched over a shopping cart. All of Columbia University lay just up there. But surely she'd avoid pushing the cart that far uphill.

Down a block was a pizza place. He'd go in and have a slice and a beer and try to figure out what to do. He had to have a plan. He couldn't just wander aimlessly over the whole Upper West Side.

A gaggle of Japanese tourists flowed down the broad steps of St. John, moving toward a parked bus. He stopped to let them pass. Several of them turned back to take pictures of the cathedral facade bathed in the glow of the fading sun. Then one lowered his camera and gestured.

Hands reached for cameras. Voices exclaimed in high, fluting staccato. Grinning photographers scrambled for angles.

Orsine looked where they aimed. When he saw what had prompted this orgy of photography, he froze. On the top step, humble and incongruous against the richly carved stone doorway, was a rusty shopping cart. Rags spilled from its top.

He had to wait three full minutes for the Japanese to finish taking pictures of this oddity at the American cathedral. When they went down the steps to queue up for their bus, he darted up.

The cart was empty.

He looked up at the immense front of St. John the Divine. She was in there, and she'd taken Ricky with her. He had them!

"We're closing, sir."

"What!"

A uniformed guard was unfastening the latches that held back the huge outer doors. "Five o'clock. Closing time, sir. We open again at seven tomorrow morning."

The great doors shut in his face.

THIRTY-THREE

"FEELING BETTER?"

Linda nodded. A glass of wine had brought color back to her face, and for the first time Mike saw a faint smile curve her mouth. Then it vanished. "We have to talk," she said.

"Want to talk here?"

"Let's go back to my apartment. I'll make us coffee."

Mike nodded to the waiter to bring the check. He was still elated that Linda had agreed to have dinner with him. He had not asked her what he wanted to know about Lorna, but he had gained her trust.

They walked the blocks back to her apartment in silence, but it was a silence without strain. He'd been able to make her understand that he had a compulsion to find her sister's killer. He might never tell her that his compulsion came from frustration that his own sister's rapist had not been caught. The other emotion that was dawning on him was his feeling for her. He might never be able to tell her that, either. But she trusted him. That would have to be enough for now.

While Linda made coffee, Mike examined the books on her living room shelves, smiling at the familiarity of the titles. When she came in with the coffee on a tray, he said, "You're a reader."

"An English major."

"We took the same courses."

She did not smile. She poured the coffee, handed him cream and sugar, and sat down where she had sat on Monday night. When she brought her cup to her lips, Mike could see her hand shaking. She was dreading this interview as much as she had dreaded that one. He could only admire her courage in being willing to talk to him now.

He was relieved that she was the one who began. "What did Kathy tell you about Lorna?"

"That she was standoffish with boys and afraid of men."

"And Gertrude?"

"She felt that Lorna was too controlled. That much self-restraint, she thought, could be the result of trauma. The deaths of your parents, so close together, could have been the shock Lorna never got over."

Linda nodded. "It's true that Lorna changed greatly when we knew how ill Daddy really was. She'd been so lively, so fun-loving, even rebellious at twelve. I don't think I could have handled her if she'd stayed that way, if I'd had to discipline and counsel her through her teens. But she never gave me a moment's worry. She helped with the housework, she shopped and cooked. She did her homework, got good grades, and never stayed out late."

"Did she seem sorry to leave Brooklyn? She had friends there."

"She showed absolutely no regret. For both of us it was a relief to get away from the house, which was far too big for the two of us, and to leave those memories behind." She looked around the room. "I have to move on again—soon. This place is too full of Lorna's death. I don't know how I'm going to bring myself to go through her things."

"Don't rush it, Linda. It hasn't been a week yet." He could tell her that those memories would never be wholly left behind, but he suspected that she knew that. Her mind was still trying to deny her loss and reject the horror of Lorna's death.

Once again she helped him. "I feel so powerless—if I could only *do* something."

He hunched forward on the couch, facing her, and said, "Maybe you can. Tell me—after you left Brooklyn you stopped going to St. Paul's—did you go to church anywhere else?"

"No, we both stopped going altogether. Church lost all meaning for me. I don't know why Lorna stopped. She never told me. I assumed she felt the same way I did. She was confirmed just before Daddy died. She knew that was something he wanted."

"Did she join any clubs or groups after she left Luther League?"

"Who told you she'd been in the Luther League?"

"Reinhardt Schmidt."

"Oh? What else did he tell you?"

Mike hesitated. If he told her how sick and suggestive Schmidt's attitude had been, her disillusion with her pastor might be the last straw. Finally he said, "Remember the story 'Lorna—Another Look'? You thought I wrote it?"

"Those filthy insinuations came from Pastor Schmidt!" She sat up and put her coffee cup down angrily. "I know he told you she was 'fun-loving' but I had no idea he'd—"

She was angry. Good. Better anger than grief. It made it easier for him to say, "He told me that Lorna was quite different from you."

"That's true. She was the family extrovert. I was the serious one."

"He also said that Lorna had 'matured' early. By that he meant her physical development."

Linda made a grimace of distaste. "What business was that of his? But that's true, too. Lorna was ahead of most girls her age."

"Those two ideas, an outgoing personality and an early sexual maturity, put together with a certain slant added up to just what you didn't want written about Lorna. I didn't put any of it in my story, but Schmidt also talked to a reporter from the *Post*. After I quit, my editor sent Ed Sheely to interview Schmidt. Ed wrote 'Another Look.'"

"You quit your job! Why?"

"I couldn't cover this story my editor's way. I don't regret quitting. It was my choice."

"I've made a mess of things, Mike," she said sadly. "I'm so sorry I didn't trust you."

"If anyone's made a mess, I have. Maybe I could have written the story differently—used Schmidt's comments without his suggestion that—"

"That Lorna was the kind of girl who asked for it! Is *that* what Schmidt said?"

Mike was startled by her awareness. And worried, too. If this was a wild goose chase, he was going to wound her to no purpose. And if he was pursuing a truth still hidden in his half formed theory, she was in for a much deeper shock.

"He was critical of women who exposed themselves to needless risk by walking in Central Park."

"Lively, fun-loving, physically mature, and flirting with danger by walking in the park! That's what Schmidt said about Lorna!"

Mike nodded unhappily. "More or less."

"It's so unfair!" she cried. "He never saw her after we left Brooklyn. Even he must have seen how she changed that year Daddy was ill. She was so unhappy. We both were. And we tried hard to help Mom."

"Did you ever think that Lorna's unhappiness was more than a natural sign of grief?"

She was silent for so long that he was sure he'd touched something she didn't want to look at. Finally she said, "What else did Pastor Schmidt say about Lorna?"

"Nothing you probably don't already know. He said her faith was strong and genuine at the time she was confirmed."

Linda didn't look at him. Her tone, when she went on, was guarded, her words tentative. "He said something to me after the funeral, something I was too tired to ask him to explain. He said he'd counseled Lorna, and that she'd accepted the Lord's mercy. At the time I thought he meant that Lorna had accepted Daddy's illness and death. But now I wonder if it could have been something else—something personal."

Easy, Mike wanted to say. He was so tense he was almost holding his breath.

"I know Pastor Schmidt had very old-fashioned ideas about propriety," she went on, "but I had no idea they went that far. I scolded Lorna once for helping herself to my makeup. She went off to Luther League looking more sixteen than twelve. With his weird 'slant' on women, he may have scolded her, too, made her feel bad about herself. It was only a few days later that Mom broke it to us about Daddy. Lorna changed. She was always pretty, but she stopped making anything of her looks. She became—well, chaste is the word, if that means anything nowadays. No more makeup. No sweaters unless they were loose and baggy. Her only vanity was wanting her legs to be tan when summer came. That quick-tan lotion was the only real cosmetic Lorna used. That's funny—"

"What's funny about wanting tanned legs?"

"That lotion—you don't use it, do you?"

"Me! Do I look as if I do? Want to see my legs?"

She almost smiled. "No, but for some reason I associate it with you. I was going through the bathroom cabinet this afternoon when Gertrude called. I'd smelled it on someone recently. You or someone near you—I'm sure of it!"

"That's impossible. I've never used the stuff. And you've seen me only twice before. The night I interviewed you and the day of the funeral."

"That's when it was. Here—after the funeral. It was so hot and close with all those people in this little space. I could smell cologne and shaving lotion, and I smelled this tanning lotion on someone. It's got a distinctive odor that remains on the skin long after it's been applied. At first I thought it was an aftershave, but as soon as I opened the bottle this afternoon, I knew that's what I'd smelled. Wait, I'll get it."

In a moment she was back with the small white bottle. She uncapped it and handed it to him. He sniffed. "Doesn't remind me of anything. You're sure it was someone in the crowd here Thursday?"

"Positive. Is it important?"

"It stuck in your mind for some reason. Do you remember seeing anyone with a good tan?"

"There was a man—I didn't hear his name—who had a dark complexion."

"What did he look like?"

"It's so hard to picture him. Dark hair. Glasses with tinted lenses."

"You didn't know him?"

"No, but there were so many people I didn't know. Lorna's friends from way back. Some curiosity-seekers, in spite of the efforts of the police to keep them out."

"And one reporter. Ex-reporter, I mean."

She smiled faintly. "Yes, he got in."

"Did this dark-haired stranger say anything?"

"He said he'd known Lorna. And he was sorry. Then he left."

"Was this before or after you chewed me out for crashing in?"

"Before. I'm almost sure."

"Lorna bought this lotion because she wanted her legs tan. And you smelled it on this man. Now why would a man use it?"

"To keep up a fading summer tan."

"That's the most obvious reason. Why else?"

"If he'd been sick, a tan would make him look healthier."

"Any other reasons?"

"To blend in brown spots. To even up a blotchy complexion. A tan makes bad skin less noticeable."

"Oh, my God!" In his agitation, Mike jumped to his feet.

"Mike, what is it?"

"Suppose he was a man with a beard?"

"He wasn't. He was clean-shaven. I'm positive."

"He'd *had* a beard. He'd just shaved it off. When a man with a good tan shaves off his beard, the lower part of his face is lighter than the top. He might have used tanning lotion to even it."

The truth hit her. She was on her feet, too, and her eyes were staring wildly. "Here? He was here? The man who—? I shook hands with him?"

"Easy," he said. "We're just guessing. We can't know yet."

"But I saw him! If he's the man, I can identify him if I can only remember what he looks like!"

"Don't try too hard. Here, sit down. Relax." She sat down where she'd been before, and he sat beside her this time. "Just relax, Linda. Close your eyes. Let it come back to you."

He watched her lean back against the cushions and shut her eyes. When her eyelids had stopped fluttering and her breathing had slowed, he began, "It's Thursday afternoon. It's been a long, sad day. You're tired. It's hot and stuffy in here. The room is full of people, and they're still crowding in. You shake hands, one after another. You thank people for coming, for expressing their sympathy. It goes on and on. Don't try to remember. Just tell me who you see."

"I see—"

"Whose hand are you shaking now?"

"Kathy. Kathy Rosen. She tells me Lorna was a sweetheart an angel. She starts to cry."

"Then who?"

"Gertrude Simonson. She tells me how bad she feels that she was the one who helped Lorna get the job looking after Ricky."

"Who's next?"

"A man with a tan. Metal-rimmed glasses, very stylish. I can't see his eyes very well because the lenses are tinted, but I know they're dark."

"Is he big? Taller than you?"

"A lot taller. He's heavyset. His hair is dark and it's combed back from his face. Slicked down."

"Anything else you notice about him?"

"His hand is sweaty."

"Anything about his voice that you remember?"

"It's strained, as if he had a cold. He mumbles something about Lorna—'a long time ago'—'sorry'—"

"That's all he says?"

She opened her eyes. "I remember now. Pastor Schmid called to me just then, over the crowd, telling me I should get some coffee and food. I looked in his direction. When I turned around again, the man was gone. He'd just turned around and left. You must have bumped into him at the door. I'm sure you came in next."

Mike shook his head. "I vaguely remember that someone big pushed past me, but I didn't look at him. I didn't look at any one, Linda, but you."

"Oh." Her eyes did not meet his.

"I want you to know."

She glanced at him quickly, then looked down again. "Mike, don't waste your time with me. I don't think I'll ever get over this, ever want anything. You have to know that."

"I won't say anything more."

She was silent, her head still down, her eyes on her hands laced in her lap. When she looked up she said, "Let's go back to this man I saw. He left right away, didn't go to the table for food. Why not?"

"He wasn't hungry?"

"Or he was claustrophobic and the crowd was too much for him."

"Or he didn't see anyone he knew except you? Now that you've got his image in your mind, is he someone you've seen before?"

"I don't think so."

"A man changed so much—older, heavier—that you don't recognize him?"

"It's such an impossibly long shot, Mike."

"We've so little to go on we have to explore every possibility, no matter how unlikely it seems."

"And even if he is the man who killed Lorna, he must be truly insane to have come here. Suppose we do find him and confront him, do you actually think he'd confess?"

"Do you want to hear my theory?"

"I didn't know you had one."

"I have. But first, I've got to ask you something. Did Lorna ever say anything to you about having bad dreams?"

She was silent for a few seconds. "Recently?"

"Yes. In the last few weeks."

"Not about dreams. But she did say one morning that she'd had a bad night. She was worried about a paper she was writing. Why?"

He told her then about Jeanette Ruiz. About Lorna's words—"It was a dream I used to have, but I haven't dreamed it in a long time."

"Oh, no!" She looked away. Her face looked old, stricken. "She *did* have nightmares."

"They started when Daddy was so sick. She'd wake up crying, hysterical. We shared a bedroom. I'd try to comfort her because I didn't want to worry Mom. We'd both cry ourselves to sleep again."

"You assumed those nightmares came from grief?"

"What else?"

"Fear. Guilt."

Linda got up. She put the empty coffee cups onto the tray, collected the cream and sugar. "I don't want to hear your theory," she said.

Mike stood up and faced her. "Listen to me, Linda. I think Lorna was raped and killed by a man who knew her. I think she saw him in the park and didn't recognize him, but subconsciously she knew who he was. That brought up the old nightmare, the same one she had when your father was ill. When, according to you, her personality changed overnight."

She picked up the tray and walked out to the kitchen. He followed. She set the tray down on the counter. Her back was to him. Her body was stiff, rigid. "No more! I don't want to hear any more! Nothing can help Lorna now!"

"But you can help yourself, Linda, if you let yourself follow this through. I haven't told you yet—the police have found a blue running suit. It was thrown away in the park Monday night. I talked to García just before I came over here."

"No!"

"He's real, Linda. If he's the man who came here Thursday, you *can* identify him. García still thinks this a random crime, but I don't."

"It has to be a random crime! It has to!"

"Why?"

"Because if it isn't, I could have prevented it!"

"How, for God's sake?"

"By making Lorna tell me what troubled her. By listening. By being open with her. If there was a man she was afraid of, I should have known! I could have—"

Certainty was growing in him now. And excitement. "Not you, Linda. Someone else."

"Who?"

"Remember we said the man might not have stayed for coffee on Thursday because he didn't see anyone he knew? Maybe it was just the opposite. Maybe he *did* see someone he knew, and he didn't want that person to see him."

"I have the guest book people signed at the funeral," she said. "We could call them and ask if they remember a dark man who might, recently, have had a beard."

"Only one person, Linda. He was moving toward you, calling to you over the crowd. The man shaking your hand would have seen him, or at least heard his voice."

"Pastor Schmidt!"

"I think we should have a talk with your former pastor."

"What are we going to say to him?"

"We'll ask him if he knows the man you'll describe. We'll ask him if he has any idea what turned a lively, fun-loving girl into a woman under such a weight of guilt that she never wanted to be sociable again or to make herself look pretty."

"You think he knows something about Lorna that she didn't tell me."

"Yes, I do."

"He might not want to tell me now. He might think he was betraying her confidence."

"You're her sister. You have a right to know." If she could bear to know. He was afraid now that things were moving too fast.

"When shall we go to see him?"

"Now, if you think you want to."

"It's Saturday night. He'll be working on his sermon."

"We'll chance it." They might, Mike thought grimly, give the Reverend Schmidt something to preach about.

THIRTY-FOUR

LINDA MEYERS' NOTE, crumpled into a ball, landed with a thump on the coffee table. Rowland had thrown it.

"How can you be so unreasonable?" Pat cried.

"That woman is after something. Forgiveness. Absolution. She sounds like a fanatic."

"You're the one who sounds like a fanatic, Rowland! Please read it again. She seems wholly concerned for us."

"No thank you. One reading is enough." Rowland was trembling so visibly that the ice cubes rattled in the glass he was holding.

García, sitting on a couch across from the Fosters, read the signs. Rowland was coming to the end of the rigid control he'd shown during the six days the detective had known him. He was going to break. García felt deeply sorry for this man who masked his fear with anger. He felt sorrier for his wife.

Pat picked up the note and smoothed the paper. "We've shared a tragedy. She seems to be a woman of great sensitivity," she said. "I'd like to meet her."

"Naive. That's what you are, Pat. That woman's sister's folly has cost us dearly. Linda Meyers knows that. She's written to try to assuage her guilt."

"I know Linda Meyers," García said, "and I can assure you she's no fanatic. What she's written comes from genuine sympathy for both of you."

Crash! Rowland's glass met the wall beside the fireplace and shattered. Glass, ice, and liquid flew. Rowland got stiffly to his feet and left the room.

Pat was on her knees, picking up pieces of glass. Silent tears rolled down her face. García moved to help her. He felt a sharp pain in his gut. This case would give him an ulcer. Pat, he knew, was in an agony of guilt and fear. But she was the stronger of the two. Rowland was becoming irrational. García, who had seen too many family tragedies, feared that if this husband and wife did not move to comfort each other soon, their marriage was doomed, whether or not Ricky was ever found.

"I'm sorry you had to witness this scene," Pat said. "Poor Rowland! He can't accept that we may never see Ricky again. He has to blame someone, so he blames me."

"Go to him. I'll finish cleaning this up."

"I can't do anything for him. I've tried. Maybe when we finally know for sure—"

She got to her feet with the broken glass in her hands and went out to the kitchen. When she came back, her hands were full of wadded paper towels. She wiped up the spilled liquid and ice cubes. "Can I get you a drink, Detective García?" she asked.

"No thank you."

When she returned from the kitchen, her tears had stopped. She was composed. She sat down again. "I want to thank you," she said.

"For what? I have no hope to give you."

"You've been kind. Tactful. I sense your understanding of what's going on between Rowland and me. I know you're doing everything you can to find Ricky."

Her words moved him. But they also frustrated him. He didn't have enough insight. He didn't have enough men. Missing children were the most difficult of missing persons to trace. They were small, inarticulate, and powerless. He had to put his faith in procedures, and they just weren't enough.

Harold Bloor's death was another nagging puzzle. It looked like the consequence of a robbery. But the door to the old man's apartment was unlocked. He'd let someone in. Or someone had followed him in, easy enough to do to an old man in a wheelchair. Had Harold Bloor died because he, the detective in charge of this case, had made a fatal error of judgment? Should he have assigned a man to watch Bloor instead of trusting the old man to stay put?

"So, what brings you here tonight?" Incredibly, Rowland was back. In his hand was a fresh glass, and he was directing the question at García.

"I have new information," said García. "The man who supplied us with the description of the man in blue is dead."

"Now maybe you'll tell us who he was!"

"His name was Harold Bloor. He was an old man, confined to a wheelchair. He went to the park daily. Became friendly with Lorna and Ricky."

"Ricky's 'Mister Boo!'" cried Pat.

"He was killed?"

"No, he died of a heart attack. He had a history of heart trouble. We think he surprised a burglar in his apartment and that the shock triggered the attack. His wallet is missing. He was lying on the floor in front of the wheelchair. When we checked for fingerprints, we found that surfaces had been wiped, even the john handle. We don't usually check for prints in an off-the-street burglary, but he was a witness in a murder investigation, however slender his evidence."

"And even less useful now that he's dead, isn't that true?" Rowland said sarcastically. "Your man in blue seems to have been nothing but an old man's pipe dream."

"We found him dead when we went to get him to look at a lineup. This morning we picked up a man who was wearing a blue running suit he claims he pulled from a trash can in the park on Monday night, near the place we found Lorna."

Wild hope leaped into Pat's face. He could hardly look at it. "There *is* a man in blue!"

"We're getting closer," García said, but he could not meet the eyes of either of Ricky Foster's parents.

THIRTY-FIVE

"I HAVE no time tonight, Mr. Marlowe. You will have to come back tomorrow."

Mike moved aside. In the darkness on the step below him, Linda came into Schmidt's view. She had suggested that they not call to ask if he would see them.

"Linda, what are you doing here? Is something wrong?"

"I need to see you, Pastor."

"Of course, my dear. But can't it wait? I'm in a situation we ministers hate to admit—I haven't prepared my sermon for tomorrow."

"Just a few minutes. Please."

Schmidt stepped back and held the door open for them. His lips were tightly compressed. He was not even trying to conceal his reluctance. In the dark study, lit only by the old-fashioned green-globed lamp, he motioned them to sit. He sank into his chair with a deep sigh. An open Bible and a blank yellow pad attested to the unwritten sermon.

He folded his hands on the desk and leaned forward with a tight smile. He nodded toward Mike. "I'm really quite surprised, Linda, to see you here with Mr. Marlowe. When we talked on Thursday, you expressed considerable hostility toward him. I take it you've been able to forgive him?"

"Yes, Pastor, I understand now, and I've asked him for his support. He has encouraged me to speak to you tonight."

"Well, what can I do for you?" Schmidt's eyes fell briefly to the yellow pad.

"On Thursday after the funeral, you told me that you had counseled Lorna and that you knew she believed in the Lord's mercy when she was confirmed. I want to know what you counseled her about."

Schmidt said nothing for a few minutes. Then, "I will say only that she was troubled. She felt some responsibility for your father's illness."

"Why? Surely she knew she didn't give him cancer!"

"No, but psychiatrists are saying there's some evidence that cancer originates in the emotions."

"Are you suggesting that something Lorna did caused Daddy's cancer?"

"No, Linda, you must not misinterpret my words. I'm only suggesting that your father's anxiety about her could have been a factor in his illness."

Linda's eyes on Schmidt were direct and clear. Mike felt a rush of admiration. "Why did you think Daddy was anxious about Lorna?"

Schmidt lifted the yellow pad and put it down again, shifted the position of the Bible. "Linda, this is really not a time for this discussion. If you'll make an appointment to see me one day next week, we can sit down and talk at length. I know I can set your mind at rest without breaking your sister's confidence. Even though she's gone, I feel that she would want that trust kept."

Mike moved in his chair. He was ready to speak, but Linda was ahead of him. "Now, Pastor. I want to know now."

"What do you want to know?" His tone was resigned.

"What you think Lorna did that was so terrible she caused Daddy to develop cancer."

"I did not mean to imply a cause-and-effect relationship there, Linda. I'm sorry I gave you that impression."

"Then what did you mean? I want to know what you counseled her about. Was it a spiritual problem? Or was it personal?"

"Both, you might say. But I can assure you, Linda, that your sister's mind was at peace when she was confirmed. She had passed through some heavy trials and come out stronger."

"You're evading, Pastor." Almost the instant the words were out of his mouth, Mike regretted them. He was going to ruin everything with his impatience.

"Mike, please!" Linda half-turned to him, then back to Schmidt with a gesture of apology. "Mr. Marlowe is a reporter and perhaps a little overeager to get facts."

"He's not here tonight for his newspaper, I hope!"

"No, no. He's here with me because I want his support. If I hadn't been so exhausted the other night, I would have asked you to tell me more. I want to know everything I can about Lorna's emotional state—her spiritual state, as you might call it. It would mean so much to me that you had helped her when she needed it—" Her voice, which had been strong and clear when she started, now broke. She fumbled in her pocketbook, then reached toward Mike, groping. He handed her his handkerchief. She put it to her eyes.

"My dear," said Schmidt sadly. "I so wish you had not come on this errand. What you want to know can only deepen your grief. You must believe that Lorna knew that the Lord was merciful, and that he forgives all our sins."

Linda's face was hidden by Mike's handkerchief. Her voice was muffled. "Sins? What sins did Lorna commit that needed to be forgiven?"

Schmidt was silent. Mike felt his nerves stretch—waiting.

"Your sister was a very beautiful girl, Linda," Schmidt said finally. The sadness in his voice was deep now.

Linda's face came up out of the handkerchief. Her eyes were not wet. "I don't understand. You're saying that her being beautiful was a sin?"

"Not her beauty. But what went with it—her responsibility for it, and for her emerging womanliness." The sadness had left Schmidt's voice now. He was plainly uncomfortable.

"How could Lorna's changing from a girl to a woman be sinful?"

"Let's just say that her judgment had not kept pace with her physical development."

"You're talking about her sexuality, aren't you, Pastor? And about the way she used it? Or showed it?"

Again Mike marveled at her courage. He could only guess what it was costing her.

Schmidt moved in his chair. "Since you put it that way, Linda—yes, that's what I mean."

"She attracted attention."

Schmidt nodded, with some relief evident in his face. "I am truly sorry, Linda. I would not have told you this if you had not forced it from me. Not after the terrible way she died."

"She made trouble at the Luther League—that's it, isn't it? And you told her that her behavior made Daddy sick? Or that it was a judgment on her?"

"She was creating havoc among the boys who came to the meetings. I could not stand by and watch them behave foolishly just to get her attention. I told her about your father's illness, impressed upon her the need for self-control so that she didn't grieve him further. She was deeply moved. She knelt down—right there—and prayed aloud for forgiveness. You saw for yourself how much she changed. That was the mark of her repentance. I would like to believe that it was lasting."

Linda had hidden her face again. She was silent. Too silent. Mike didn't know how she kept from screaming.

"Forgive me, sir, for the impatience I showed earlier," he said. "I need to ask you something. Ignorant as I am of 'spiritual matters,' I do know the sins you're attributing to Lorna are ones not usually committed alone. Was there a particular boy who was attracted to her?"

Schmidt stiffened. "They all were. To single out one boy would invite a most dangerous kind of speculation."

"One a little bolder than the rest? More persistent?"

The minister's fingers beat a rapid tattoo on the arms of his chair. "If you had any sense of fitness, Mr. Marlowe, you would not ask that question. When I first met you, I believed you sincere. I thought that, unlike many media people, you were sensitive to the feelings of others—to their rights. I expected you to respect my professional ethics. But your ill-advised meddling is changing my opinion of you. I don't know what 'support' you think you're giving Linda by putting her through this tonight. If this is an attempt to get information that you can wrench out of context for your paper—you'll be the one in need of forgiveness!"

Mike looked quickly at Linda. She was still bent over, still covering her face with her hands. His anxiety for her almost stopped him. But they were so close to the truth. If he stopped hammering at Schmidt now, the man would go behind the wall of clerical privilege. They would never find out.

Schmidt was speaking earnestly to Linda's bowed head. "I have said too much, Linda. We will not speak of this again. You may, however, be assured that Lorna knew forgiveness when I confirmed her. Then you and she left this parish, and I did not see her again until she was lying in her coffin."

Linda did not stir. Her silent anguish was more than Mike could bear. He knew that she was so beaten down now that she was powerless.

It was up to him. He had to take a very big chance. He let the silence in the room go on until Linda's pain and the minister's tension were almost palpable.

"Lorna was young. Pretty. Turning into a woman," he said.

Schmidt looked surprised. Then he nodded briefly.

"Lively. Enticing. Looked a lot older than she was."

Another nod. And a deepening frown.

"With that kind of personality and that ripening young body, she must have been dynamite at the Luther League!"

A dull red washed up into Schmidt's sallow cheeks. "Why are you doing this?"

"Are you sure, Pastor, that it wasn't *you* on whom Lorna cast her spell?"

The red faded from Schmidt's face. Even his lips went white. "You dare!" he said in a hoarse whisper. "You dare! Get out! Get out at once! Linda, get this man out of here. How could you have mixed yourself up with anyone so crude, so insensitive—"

"Come off it, Schmidt! Admit that you lusted after her! What did she do to you, seduce you in the Sunday School?"

"No! Not I—" He stopped as if he'd been choked.

"Who? Who was it, Schmidt?"

"Get out!"

"Who was the boy who grew up with an insatiable lust for Lorna Meyers? Who raped her, then killed her? And to make sure no one witnesses his terrible deed, killed the child who was with her? Are you going to give us his name?"

All three of them were on their feet now. Schmidt's mouth was working—choking sounds came from his throat and he was shaking with violent rage.

Linda reached blindly for Mike. "I've got to get out of here!"

"We're leaving," said Mike. "But you—" He looked at Schmidt's livid face. "I'm going straight to the police with this. García will want to know whom you're shielding. You better be ready with answers for him!"

He put his arm around Linda, who was stumbling toward the door. He looked back. Schmidt was staring after them. His blanched face was wet with sweat and his eyes were glassy.

THIRTY-SIX

SCHMIDT FELL BACK into his chair. His breath came in gasps and his whole body shook. Anger. He'd shown anger. Worse. He'd lost control. Let Marlowe see. Marlowe...vile... insulting.:.his insinuation...filthy...

Lorna— No. He would not remember Lorna.

He took out his handkerchief and wiped his face. His hands still shook. He pushed away the Bible, the pad.

He'd said too much. Marlowe had tricked him. He had to pull himself together. Think. Marlowe's theory about the man who killed Lorna. It was absurd. Irresponsible. And just plausible enough to be wildly dangerous.

Maybe it was only a guess. Maybe only a cheap trick to wring information from him, information he could use to write a story full of distortions and innuendo. Maybe Marlowe was only guessing.

But if the police believed it, followed up—

He couldn't ignore Marlowe's threat. He returned the handkerchief to his pocket and held his hands still on the arms of his chair, trying to control their trembling.

He could not ignore Marlowe's threat because he could not rid his mind of a single, nagging image. The back **of a** man's head. He had seen it Thursday afternoon when the man shouldered his way out of Linda's apartment.

Bob Orsine.

The glimpse had been so quick. He could be wrong. His coupling of Bob Orsine with Lorna Meyers had made him see in a stranger's slick, dark head the boy now grown to manhood. He had not seen Bob for ten years. Not since that night.

Bob Orsine. Clumsy, tongue-tied, awkward. Schmidt had been shy and tall for his age himself; he understood. He'd done his best to draw Bob out, gave him responsibilities, made him head acolyte. Nothing had helped. The boy remained out of place, too old for the Luther League youngsters, without friends his own age.

He'd watched the boy's dumb infatuation with Lorna. The girl had led him on. Bob was too naive to see how indiscriminately Lorna bestowed the warmth of her personality. She was just as Marlowe had said she was—enticing.

He'd done the right thing. He'd saved Bob from the terrible stigma that lies and rumors would have fastened upon a boy so large and so uncouth. He'd breathed his thanks a few months later when he'd heard that Bob had gone into the service. The Army would mature him, teach him skills he could use when he got out.

The back of a man's head. Thick dark hair, greased and combed close to his skull. Bob could have come back here to live after he left the service. He could have read about Lorna's death in the paper and come to pay his respects. But if the man really was Bob, why hadn't he waited to speak to his former pastor?

Barbara D'Onofrio, Bob's sister, still lived in the neighborhood. He looked at his watch. It was late for a pastoral call, but he had to act. If Marlowe did go to the police, Bob could become the object of a manhunt. He might have to save Bob again.

THIRTY-SEVEN

"WHADDYA WANT with Bob?" Barbara D'Onofrio pushed a tangle of gray-streaked hair back from her forehead and looked suspiciously at Schmidt. Her dark eyes were like her brother's. From the room behind her he could hear the drone of the TV.

Schmidt schooled himself to patience. "I apologize, Mrs. D'Onofrio, for calling on you at this hour. I haven't heard anything about Bob in such a long time, and, as I was in the neighborhood tonight, I thought I'd stop to inquire."

"He don't live with us. He's got a room in the city."

"Then he did come back to the city after he got out of the service?"

"Not right away. He was out west a long time. Just got back here a coupla months ago. He's got a job with a messenger service. Goes all over town. And, like I said, he's got a room in Manhattan."

Schmidt did not want to continue the conversation while he was standing on the front steps. Although the windows all along the row of attached houses all seemed to be closed, he did not want to take a chance on being overheard. "Could I trouble you, Mrs. D'Onofrio, for a glass of water?"

Her sullen face become contrite. "Sorry, Pastor, I shoulda invited you in sooner. Truth is, I'm kinda embarrassed I ain't been to church in so long. My husband, he's Catholic, and—"

"I quite understand, and I haven't come to scold you."

He followed her into the living room. She snapped off the TV and scooped up a pile of newspapers from a chair. Every table in the room had a smudged glass, a stained coffee cup, an overflowing ashtray. Dust rolls fringed the rug. He could remember when the homes he visited in the parish of St. Paul's smelled of furniture polish and freshly ironed linen.

"Make yourself comfortable, Pastor. Could I get you a cup of coffee? My husband, Joey, he's workin' late tonight."

"Coffee would be welcome, if it isn't too much trouble."

The coffee was instant. With it was a plate of bakery muffins. He ignored the sticky sugar bowl, the powdered creamer, and sipped his coffee black.

"Tell me about Bob," he said, forcing a comfortable heartiness into his voice. "I've heard nothing about him since he went into the Army, and that was years ago."

She helped herself to a muffin and put one on a paper napkin in front of him. "Actually, Pastor, it's a real coincidence you comin' here today askin' about Bob."

"Why is that?"

"He was just here the other night. Thursday."

"Is that so unusual?"

"I'll say it is! Weeks go by and we don't see nothin' of Bob. Then all of a sudden he just drops in at dinner time."

"You hadn't invited him for dinner?"

"We invite him all the time, but he don't come. I even gave him a house key so he'd feel like it was his place again. I don't think he's ever used it. Then all of a sudden he's here. Looked real good. Wearin' a suit. Hair combed real nice. He'd even gotten rid of that beard."

Schmidt set his coffee cup down carefully. "Beard?"

"Yeah, he said when he got out of the Army, he was so sick of the scalpin' they gave him he wasn't never gonna cut his hair or shave again. He did look a sight! Like one of them hippies! But I guess they all look that way out on the west coast."

"Did he shave it off recently?"

"He didn't say. He still had it when he came back here a coupla months ago. And like I said, we didn't see him in a while."

"How long was Bob on the west coast?"

"He stayed out there after the Army—after he left the Army. Six, seven years maybe. Then he was in Texas awhile and Colorado. We thought he was gonna settle down out there. We was surprised when he came back."

"What did Bob do while he was living out there?"

"Different jobs, I guess. Bob wasn't much for writing letters. But he'd told us he tried different things—construction, driving a cab, pumping gas. Now he's got this job as a messenger. He says he don't like to be cooped up. He likes to move around.''

"He served in Vietnam?"

"Yeah, he don't like to talk about it, though."

"That must have been a terrible experience for Bob."

"What experience? What are you talking about?" Her voice was sharp and her face had lost its affability.

Surprised, he said, "I was thinking of the danger, the lack of support for the war from people here, the rigor of Army discipline—"

"What are you after, Pastor? Why are you snooping? You wanna find out about Bob, you go ask him. What happened between him and the Army is his business!"

He was dismayed. "I'm truly sorry. I didn't mean to pry. If something unpleasant is connected with Bob's service record, you're absolutely right that it's none of my business."

Barbara was silent, fidgeting with the spoon, then unnecessarily stirring the cold coffee. In her tired, angry face, he saw defensiveness fade, replaced by a wistful anxiety. If he had not been so revolted by her slovenliness, he might have felt sorry for her.

"You know how close-mouthed Bob always was," she said finally.

"Yes, I remember. He was very quiet."

"He ain't changed. All I know is, the girl lied. It wasn't his fault. She asked for it."

"What!"

"The one they said, you know, he attacked, the one they discharged him for."

"This happened while he was in the service?"

"Yeah. She was a—excuse me, Pastor—a prostitute. I hope you won't think bad of Bob. I mean, he's a man. I know it ain't right, his goin' to one of them houses, but he was in Vietnam in that god-awful war, an' he needed—" Her face was scarlet.

"Never mind that. Go on."

"He said she was willing. She took his money—that meant he was willing, don't it? Next thing she's screamin' he's beating her up. The MPs come and they rough Bob up—next thing the Army is giving him a discharge. Mental, they said. Battle

fatigue made him crazylike. But that whore, she musta lie
Bob wasn't like that.''

"I remember Bob as a teenager, coming to the Luth
League. He was so shy, so terrified of girls.''

She leaned forward. Her eyes sought his eagerly. "He wa
like that, wasn't he? He couldn't have changed so much, coul
he? That girl that he got discharged for—she was lying. Bo
was afraid to touch a girl, let alone try anything—''

"Did Bob tell you where he'd been on Thursday?''

Her defenses were back. "He hadn't been nowhere. He ju
come by to have dinner with us.''

"Did you ask him why he was wearing a suit?''

"Bob don't like me asking questions, so I don't, but Joey, m
husband, he kids a lot. He asked Bob how come he was s
dressed up—did he have a date and she stood him up.''

"How did Bob take that?''

"He didn't say nothin'. But I could tell he was kinda mad. H
said he ain't been feelin' too good. He'd took a couple of day
off from work.''

"Do you have Bob's phone number? I'd like to give him
call, see him again. It's been ten years. He'll be surprised!''

"Yeah, I got it here somewhere.'' She rose to rummage in
pocketbook that dangled by its strap from the knob of the doo
leading to the kitchen. When she brought him the limp scrap o
paper, he copied the number into a notebook he carried in hi
breast pocket.

"That's one of them SROs,'' she said. "It's a pay phone
Someone answers, you ask for Bob Orsine, and they holler fo
him. If you do get to see Bob, Pastor—''

"You want me to tell him something?''

She opened her hands in a strangely helpless gesture. "I don'
know, exactly—''

He knew then how worried she was about Bob. And afraid
Aloud he said, "Would you like me to pray with you?''

Obediently she folded her hand and closed her eyes. He in
toned a blessing on her and her home. The words fell mechan
ically from his lips.

She walked with him to the door. His hand was on the knob when she said, behind him, "That girl—Lorna Meyers—the one that was killed—she used to go to St. Paul's, didn't she?"

He turned around. "Yes, I knew her and her family. I took the funeral."

"That was Thursday, wasn't it?"

"Thursday afternoon."

"Did many people from this neighborhood go to it?"

"Some. I saw a few I knew."

She would not ask if Bob was one of them. He could not say that he wasn't. Barbara might have known of Bob's lonely yearning for the young Lorna. She had surely seen in the papers the police drawing of the supposed killer. Could she really be afraid that if the concealing beard and glasses were stripped away, the face revealed would be her brother's?

Poor Bob! It was monstrous. Fear began to invade him, like a slow poison. Monstrous!

Impossible.

THIRTY-EIGHT

HE'D STRANGLED LORNA. This time he would use a knife. Th
Army had taught him that, too. It was quick and quiet.

He'd have to work fast. The old woman first. Then Ricky.

He put his knife down on the bureau and took a bite o
greasy hamburger. He washed it down with lukewarm coffee
He had to keep up his strength. He had to plan his strategy
Here in his room he was safe, but when he went out there h
had to be ready to be real smart.

Seven A.M. He had nine hours till he could get into the ca
thedral. When the doors opened, he'd be there. He'd go in lik
he was going to the early service. While he sat through it, he'
look around, check it out, keep his eyes open for likely hidin
places. After the service was over, he'd walk around like he wa
a tourist. He'd search.

Another service started at eleven it said on the board ou
front. People would be coming in early to get good seats. Th
choir would practice like it did at St. Paul's. The place woul
never really be empty. But it was so big he might not be no
ticed.

He'd never been inside. He tried to remember the sanctuar
at St. Paul's. This would be a hundred times bigger. Full o
niches and alcoves and dark places. He'd have to try to thin
like the old woman. Where would she have found a place t
hide?

Suppose she put up a fight? He'd have to make sure sh
didn't. He'd have to creep up behind her and slip it to her fast

The hamburger was suddenly tasteless in his mouth. The
what? He'd be inside. He'd have to get out, leaving two dea
bodies behind him. There was no back way out of the cathe
dral. After the doors had closed on him this afternoon, he'
walked all the way around the block looking for another wa
in. There wasn't any. The whole fucking block was walled an

fenced. There was a security guard in a glass booth at the gate to the grounds.

No way in or out except through those big front doors. Doors that opened onto Amsterdam. Onto a broad flow of stairs. Open. Exposed.

He had to look like a churchgoer. That meant a jacket. His windbreaker was gone. He hoped it wouldn't be a cold day. He had to be ready to run. That mean his running shoes. Not a great outfit for church. Would he be conspicuous?

The shoes were where he'd shoved them Monday night. He got them out of the curtained corner that served as his closet. They were stiff and smeared with mud. He held them over the wastebasket and clapped them together. Little chunks of dried dirt fell out of the grooved soles.

Suppose when he found the old bitch, she didn't have the kid with her? Suppose she'd hidden him someplace else? He'd force her to tell him. Then kill her quick. Then find the kid and kill him. Then get out of the cathedral without attracting attention.

God! He was sweating.

He'd have to get away from the West Side for a while. Cops would be all over the place once the bodies were found. It would be worse than when they were first hunting for Ricky. It would be the biggest manhunt the city had ever seen.

He'd go over to Brooklyn, stay with Barbara and Joe. give them a story about losing his place because the rent went up. Then he'd find another room. Somewhere way downtown.

After he slipped out of the cathedral, he'd go around the block to Morningside. Scramble down the cliff and into the park. He'd skirt the edge of the ballfield and come out on 110th. It was a short block from there to the subway.

Or he could cross Central Park, go over to the East Side and take the Lex downtown. That would be better. He didn't want to get trapped on a subway platform so close to the scene.

THIRTY-NINE

"I'M SORRY, LINDA! I sure blew that one!" In the back of the taxi, Mike put his arm around Linda. She didn't push him away. She had not said a word since they left Schmidt's study.

Her silence frightened him. On top of her grief, the truth of what Schmidt had done to Lorna—laying on a girl not yet into her teens an intolerable burden of sexual guilt and self-hatred—might be too much for Linda to take.

She stirred and eased herself away from him. "I'm all right," she said.

"Are you really?"

"I'll never get over it, if that's what you mean. I'll never forgive Pastor Schmidt. But I'm all right. You were great! Thank you."

"For what? All I did was make him so mad he threw us out before he told us the boy's name. Boy then, man now."

"He wouldn't have told us, no matter what you did. But we can find out."

"How?"

"I'll get hold of the names of everyone who was in the Luther League with Lorna. We'll talk to them. I'm sure a lot of them still live in this area."

"You'll do nothing of the sort! This goes to García. He'll listen to me now."

She looked out of the window of the cab. "Mike, where are we going?"

"Back to your place. I'll call García from there."

"We shouldn't be taking a cab. I can ride the subway."

"You were in no shape to ride the subway when we came out of there. So just relax."

She leaned back. Her shoulder just touched his. "Pastor Schmidt will say the same thing to García that he did to us—it's his professional right not to divulge Lorna's confidence."

"That's not legally binding. He'll fight like hell not to tell, but he'll have to. By that time, though, García will already have found out by questioning the Luther Leaguers."

"Pastor Schmidt doesn't want the man identified. He's protecting him. Why? I should think he'd want the murderer to be brought to justice."

"Linda, don't you see? He doesn't think the man is guilty. Not of rape, anyway."

"Then he does think Lorna asked for it!"

"It's himself he's protecting, Linda. I'm sure of it. He may not know it, but he identifies with that man. You were hiding in my handkerchief when I accused him of lusting after her himself. You didn't see his face. I did. And something else—the first time I talked with him he said something stupid and pious about the man who had done this awful deed needing the Lord's mercy. I thought he was just spouting clerical crap, but I can see now he may have been remembering the way Lorna affected him."

"She really wasn't like that, Mike. Not seductive, anyway. She was warm and outgoing—"

"And pretty and desirable. And some men can't handle their own feelings, so they blame women for them. Don't worry about what I think of Lorna. I know she was just as you described her."

She sat up suddenly. "Carrie!" she cried.

"Who's Carrie?"

"Carrie Braun. She lived behind us in Brooklyn. Her daughter Annie was Lorna's best friend. They went to school together, and to Luther League. After the funeral Carrie said something to me about the way Annie and Lorna used to tease the boys. Stop!" she called to the cab driver. When he pulled over she said, "We have to go back. She lives close to St. Paul's. Turn around, please. We're going someplace else."

"Make up your mind, lady."

Linda gave directions. "And please stop at the next phone booth you see." To Mike she said, "I know Carrie won't open the door at this hour unless she knows we're coming."

Carrie Braun's ample form was wrapped in a chenille bathrobe. Her plain face, devoid of makeup, was bright with unconcealed curiosity. As soon as she opened the door, Mike could smell fresh-perked coffee. Linda introduced Mike.

"I'm awful glad you think there's something I can do for you, Linda. Something you want to know? Come out to the kitchen, do you mind? Coffee's just ready."

Mike wasn't sure whether it was tension or the number of cups of coffee he'd already had today that was making his heart beat so strongly when they sat down in Carrie's spotless kitchen. The man in blue might, in the next few minutes, become a person, with a history and a name.

Linda came quickly to the point. "You reminded me the other day, Carrie, of how Annie and Lorna used to giggle together and tease the boys. I want to know the names of those boys."

"Oh, no, Linda! You can't think it was one of them!"

"I certainly hope not. But we have to try everything."

Carrie's round face was screwed up with distress. "I can't let you do this, Linda. Why, there was Georgie Anderson and Jack Bergman and the Hittner boys. Will lives just two blocks over and Dickie is out in Hampstead. I know those boys. I know their folks. Those boys aren't like that, Linda. You'll get in awful trouble if you start accusing—"

"We're not accusing, Mrs. Braun," said Mike. "The police are looking into the possibility that the man is someone who knew Lorna a long time ago. Don't you see that it's just as important that we know who it isn't as who it is?"

She looked doubtful. "I suppose so, but—"

"So we need names. Who besides George and Jack and Will and Dickie?"

"Most of those boys are married now, Linda. You'll ruin them!"

"Not all of them," said Linda. "Only one. Was there any boy that Annie said she didn't like? Or that she and Lorna were afraid of for some reason?"

Carrie's mouth fell open. "Oh, I can't believe you said that! I thought of it just this minute, Linda. There was someone. Some boy they used to make fun of because they didn't like him. What was his name?"

"Do you know anything about him? Where he lived? What he looked like?"

"You know half the time I didn't pay attention to their giggling and carrying on. It was always some boy or other. But there was one they said was real 'yucky.' You ought to ask Pastor Schmidt about him, Linda. If he was a boy in the church, Pastor would know. Of course it could have been someone from school. The neighborhood was beginning to run down then, lots of bad elements. I told Annie whenever she went out, 'Now you stay on well-lighted streets. Don't go anywhere unless you're with a crowd—'"

Linda interrupted. "Would Annie remember the name of the boy they didn't like?"

"She might. Want to call her? She's out in L.A., but it's early out there. You're welcome to use the phone."

"I'll pay for the call." Linda reached for the phone on the kitchen wall and dialed as Carrie dictated the number. After the first few minutes of conversation with Annie Braun, Linda cut across the flood of horror and sympathy and asked her question.

Annie remembered. The boy who had been the target of their dislike was an older kid. The Pastor's pet. He'd served as an acolyte in the church and he'd come to the Luther League. He was so unattractive and so awkward that no one liked him, and so big that most of them were afraid of him. She and Lorna had teased him mercilessly, but she thought Lorna felt sorry for the guy. One night, Annie remembered, she'd had to go home by herself because Lorna had been called into Pastor Schmidt's study. Lorna never told her why, but it must have been serious because Lorna was never the same after that. She got quiet and a whole lot more religious, like she'd been born again or something. Then Lorna and Linda's dad got so sick, and the girls didn't see so much of each other. Lorna had stopped coming to the Luther League, and the girls drifted apart. Annie was real sorry that happened.

Did Annie remember the name of the big kid?

She did. His name was Bob. Bob Orsine.

Linda took a deep breath. Her hand was white as she clutched the phone. "Do you know where Bob Orsine is now?"

"I haven't the faintest idea. It's been ten years! Bob stopped going to church about that same time, I think. The Luther League broke up."

"Did you ever hear anything about Bob Orsine after that?"

"I'm sorry I can't help you, Linda. I really don't know anything about him. The only thing I remember is that someone told me he'd gone into the Army and that he got sent to Vietnam."

FORTY

THE FARTHER NORTH the subway took him, the deeper became Schmidt's misgivings. Manhattan was almost terra incognita to him, its upper reaches an unimaginably hostile jungle where barbarians waited to rob and kill. Only his collar, he was sure, was keeping muggers from attacking him on the train.

Bob's voice on the phone. The familiar, husky voice, sounding so frightened. That was why he'd agreed to leave Brooklyn and meet Bob up here. As soon as he'd mentioned Lorna Meyers, the boy had begged him to come. He seemed to be near tears.

It was a long ride. And with every jerking stop and start, with every pounding mile, he had fought to keep down the memory that had been thrusting its way into his conscious mind ever since he'd heard that Lorna had been raped. He couldn't hold it back any longer.

A Sunday night meeting of the dwindling Luther League. The young ones, all except Bob under fourteen. The older teenagers were lost to the church. And among these children, he knew which ones would try to sneak cans of beer into the parish hall, who would slip out to return sleepy-eyed and reeking of marijuana.

He kept an eye on the back row of chairs where Lorna and Annie were holding court. Annie, loud and pushy, with a high screech of laughter that set his teeth on edge.

And Lorna. Lorna, who had only to enter a room to have boys scrambling over one another to get close to her. He watched one after another fall to the magic of those eyes fringed with long lashes, her smile that teased and beckoned, her light, slender but rounded young body. With distaste he saw that the fringed lashes were thick with mascara, and that her lips were the color of ripe cherries.

He would have excluded her from the Luther League if he could, but what would he say to Ruth and Harold? To Harold, especially, whose terminal cancer had just been diagnosed. Besides, he knew that Lorna's expulsion from the group would mean its demise.

Bob Orsine was "on" that night, entertaining with puppets he fashioned from a folded handkerchief. On stage he temporarily overcame the loutishness that made him the clown of the group.

After the performance the youngsters gathered around the piano for hymns and folks songs. Annie and Lorna were teasing Bob. They declared his handkerchief tricks suitable only for entertaining small children. Bob, his face red and his eyes moist, said huskily, "I'd like to show you a trick or two!"

Annie and Lorna squealed and ran from him. Schmidt's stern look quelled their mock terror and stopped the teasing, but it did not put an end to their fit of giggles. A few minutes later he saw that Annie was hanging over the piano, doing her best to distract Jack Bergman, who was trying to accompany the singing. Bob and Lorna had disappeared.

He found them in an empty Sunday School room.

The remembered image sent a wave of heat through him. He'd opened the door. The room was in darkness, but the light streaming in behind him showed the movement—caught the two bodies on the floor. He saw white legs, spread—and the boy on her—he heard the sounds—Bob's heavy grunts, Lorna's cry.

He'd shouted. They rolled apart. There were confused motions while they grabbed at clothing—adjusted—got to their feet. He told Lorna to go at once to the parsonage and wait for him in his study.

Bob cried, great hoarse sobs. "I didn't mean for this to happen, I swear I didn't, Pastor. She's so pretty! She acted like she liked me—"

Instantly Schmidt knew what the poor boy was trying to say. She'd seduced him. A boy like Bob, so shy and awkward, had no defenses against a girl like Lorna.

"Bob, a terrible thing might have happened if I hadn't come in just now."

"I know, Pastor, I know!" The overgrown boy actually had tears rolling down his face.

"A pretty unspeakable sin."

"I didn't know how it would be, Pastor! Alone here in the dark with her. She let me kiss her—and touch her—and pretty soon I couldn't stop what I was doing—"

"You must pray for strength not to fall into such temptation again."

"I will, I swear I will!"

"You will have to leave St. Paul's. I'll be sorry to lose you, Bob, but you cannot stay here where you'll continue to see Lorna Meyers."

Bob gulped. "Whatever you say, Pastor."

"You must stay away from her. That girl is no good."

"I'll never go near her again!" Bob wiped his eyes with the backs of his hands.

He had gone back to the meeting, dismissed the youngsters with a quick benediction, and crossed the lawn to the parsonage.

Lorna was in his study, sitting on the edge of the chair across from his desk. She was bent over, her arms clutched around herself and she was shivering as if she had a chill. He expected boldness, defiance, denial. Instead, she looked up at him with eyes that looked enormous in her white face. She seemed almost dazed. He was sure that her repentance had already begun.

He did not raise his voice. In a calm, quiet tone he told her that her father had incurable cancer. It was the only way to make her understand the gravity of her situation. Harold and Ruth had not wanted the girls to be told until his condition could no longer be explained away.

He'd watched her white, empty look turn to disbelief, then horror. Her mouth had moved without sound. With satisfaction he saw her slide off the chair and onto her knees.

"Don't tell Daddy! Please don't tell Daddy!" He looked down at the young, anguished face. Tears hung on her lashes, spilled over. Her breasts, as she strained her body upward, pleading, were round and soft in the sweater she was wearing.

"I won't tell him, Lorna. He'd be so grieved to know what kind of girl you've become. He may know already, just from looking at you. He may be so sick with worry about you that he has no strength to fight his dreadful illness."

She wept silently, still kneeling.

"What were you doing in that classroom with Bob?"

She looked up. Her makeup had smeared and her face was wet and blotchy. "Bob said he wanted to talk to me. I felt bad because Annie and I had teased him. He seemed so unhappy. He begged me to come with him for a few minutes to someplace where we could be alone and talk."

"Did he overpower you in the hall and drag you in?"

"No."

"And when you got into that dark room with Bob, did you let him kiss you, fondle you—"

"No! I didn't *let* him, Pastor! When we got into the room, he didn't turn on the light. He closed the door, then he grabbed me and kissed me—then he pushed me down. He said something about knowing that I wanted—" Here she stopped, shuddering. "As if I—then he began to—I tried to fight, to push him off, but he's so big—"

The warm feeling that invaded Schmidt reached his throat, made his voice deep and soft. "You don't really expect me to believe that, do you, Lorna? Surely you know that you invited what almost happened to you tonight. If I hadn't opened the door, you would have dragged not only yourself, but that poor, loveless boy into the blackest of sins."

"Pastor—" The face that looked up at him was a child's face now, and her words came high and thin. "Bob...he...he hurt me."

He leaned over her, caught the scent of her body, the perfume of her makeup. His voice was richer now and stern. "Be careful, Lorna. Don't say anything you're not willing to prove. False witness, too, is a sin."

She bent her head again and was utterly still. He could see only the top of her head and her soft, rounded body slumped in a posture of grief and contrition.

His hand went out to touch her soft curls. He spoke now in a hoarse whisper, "Lorna, you must pray." His hand on her head moved, as if by its own will, curved down to caress her cheek, rested there for a moment, then slid to her shoulder. His hand lay there lightly and then it moved again. For a second her young breast was soft and warm under his seeking fingers.

She jerked back. Her head came up.

"Pray, Lorna! Pray that you do not lead me into temptation. Pray for forgiveness, Lorna. Repent and change your ways."

She bowed again. But he had seen what was in her eyes.

She prayed.

From that night on, she was a different girl. She did not come back to the Luther League, which, as he had feared, soon ceased to exist. She came faithfully to confirmation classes, received his instruction without comment or questions, and was confirmed shortly before Harold died.

In a final counseling session with her before her confession of faith, *he* assured her that her repentance was accepted, her sin forgiven. She only looked at him in white-faced silence and turned her face away.

It was his custom at confirmation to lay his hands on the heads of the kneeling youngsters as he blessed them. When he came to Lorna, he held his hands over her head, and he did not touch her.

The train ground into the station at 110th Street. Only a handful of people got off when Schmidt did. In their sidelong glances he saw menace and distrust. Aboveground, his fellow passengers quickly dispersed. He was alone. On one side a row of shabby stores. At the corner a gas station with disemboweled automobiles on its apron. Across the street the park. Only traffic moving and stopping with the lights showed that this was a normal midnight at Frederick Douglass Circle.

He shied violently as a shadow moved out from a doorway. "Pastor?" The voice was a whisper.

"Bob? Is that you, Bob?"

"Yeah, it's me. Let's move on. This ain't a great neighborhood to hang around in. We'll go over to the park."

"The park!"

"It's OK. A lot safer than it looks. No one will see us."

Schmidt allowed himself to be escorted across the street and into the park at its northwest corner. The lighted sidewalk seemed mocked by the darkness on either side, a darkness full of the whisper of dry leaves and the swish of an occasional car going through the underpass. At each light he stole a glance at the man beside him, trying to see the face of the boy he had known.

"Thanks a lot for coming up here, Pastor. I guess you wonder why I didn't want to go to Brooklyn." The husky voice was the same as it had been the night the boy sobbed out his anger over what had happened between him and Lorna.

"I could tell that something has you worried." Schmidt was drawing a measure of comfort from the absolute normality of a playground on their right and the sound of cars on 110th Street just the other side of the wall that paralleled the walk.

"I think the cops might be looking for me. I've been laying low."

"You haven't done anything, have you, Bob?"

"No! It's just that when Lorna was killed, I was afraid someone might remember how things was between her and me, might wonder if I was the one who done it."

"What happened that night ten years ago wasn't your fault, Bob. I know that. And I'm sure no one knows about it except you and me."

"Yeah, but there was something else. While I was in the service. That wasn't my fault either. But I been afraid someone would look up my record and remember the thing with Lorna. If they put two and two together it might add up to something not too good for yours truly."

"I'm afraid someone has done just that, Bob."

Bob stopped. "Who?"

"Your sister is worried about you. That's one reason I wanted to see you tonight. I'd like to be able to tell Barbara that she doesn't need to be afraid."

"What's the other reason?"

"Linda Meyers came to see me tonight. She and that reporter, Michael Marlowe, have cooked up some scheme. They tried to threaten me. Said they were going to the police with their suspicions."

"What suspicions?"

"They think whoever killed Lorna was someone who knew her. They tried to get me to give them the names of the boys who were attracted to her."

"They were all nuts about her! No one could single me out, unless—"

"You can be absolutely certain, Bob, that no one knows of that incident. I've told no one. I'm certain that Linda doesn't know. I believe that Lorna was too ashamed of herself to tell her. And if the police pressure me, I can give them the names of half a dozen boys who made fools of themselves, fawning over her—"

"Thanks, Pastor. I'm glad I can count on you."

"Always. And I'll reassure Barbara. I'll see her tomorrow."

They were moving again, walking now along the concrete border of the Harlem Meer. A sharp breeze had risen. The dark water lapped and rippled. The East Drive was empty.

"You didn't go to Lorna's funeral, did you, Bob?"

"No! Why would I do that? I hardly knew Linda."

"I thought I saw you."

"At the funeral?"

"No, afterwards at Linda's apartment."

"Not me, Pastor!"

"I'm glad it wasn't you. It's unlikely, but there might have been someone there who recognized you, remembered that you'd been attracted to Lorna."

"The guy who killed her had a beard, the papers said."

"Surely he would have shaved it off by this time."

"Did you recognize me, Pastor? Now, I mean. After ten years?"

They were standing in a circle of light from one of the lamps. Schmidt peered at him. Bob's eyes were hidden behind the screen of his glasses. The thick hair was as he remembered it. His body was larger, bulkier, more muscular. He was no longer an overgrown boy. "No, I knew your voice, but I don't think I would have recognized you. You're a man, Bob. The Army must have done you some good, in spite of the unfair way they treated you."

"That's right. Did me a lot of good." Bob was smiling now. The light caught the gleam of his teeth, those oddly small teeth. Schmidt remembered that he'd always been embarrassed about them.

They moved from light to shadows, still skirting the dark lake.

"You wouldn't hurt anyone, I know that, Bob. I know the kind of girl Lorna was. As for the idea that you could have anything to do with that little boy's disappearance, it's absurd! I remember how good you were with the young people. How you entertained them. Do you still do those clever tricks with a handkerchief, Bob?"

FORTY-ONE

GARCÍA LOOKED DOWN at the mound of flesh that had been, maybe not even an hour ago, a middle-aged man of the cloth. Now, shivering in the wind that was blowing across the Harlem Meer, García saw the second murder in Central Park in a week. What had brought this man to such an unlikely place to be strangled with a handkerchief around his neck? A lovers' rendezvous? An unwise choice of shortcut?

Tonight another murder in Central Park. Tomorrow sixteen thousand runners. For hours and hours they'd be pouring in.

"Wallet's still on him," said the man who was examining the corpse.

"Who is he?"

"Schmidt, Reinhardt. Home address Brooklyn."

Brooklyn. Why hadn't the sucker taken his last walk in Prospect Park?

"Here's a card. St. Paul's Lutheran Church. He must've been the man there."

St. Paul's? Brooklyn? This was the minister who had buried Lorna Meyers!

Mike Marlowe was right.

FORTY-TWO

THE LIGHT WAS MERCILESS. Detective García had aged twenty years since he first questioned her about Lorna. Mike looked the way he would when he was forty. Both men's faces were dark with stubble.

She was glad that García suggested breakfast while they talked over the assortment of clues that had suddenly come together, but in the steamy warmth of the all-night restaurant, her mind was sinking into paralysis. She sipped her coffee and toyed with pieces of soggy toast and tried to follow what Mike and the detective were saying.

Reinhardt Schmidt was dead. It was hard to grasp. The man who had said he had no time to see them because he had a sermon to prepare had left his study shortly after they left him. He had been found in Central Park, where someone had knocked him out with a karate chop and strangled him with a handkerchief.

When she and Mike finally reached García with the name of Bob Orsine, García told them about Schmidt. There were gaps, but the pieces were coming together.

In the middle of the night, however, facts were hard to come by. Orsine had no criminal record. The National Personnel Records Center computer, which had his service record, if indeed he had one, would not be on-line until Monday.

Tomorrow the police would call in an artist, who would try to re-create from Linda's description the face of the man who had come to the apartment.

She had tried, but she could not remember the face of the large youth who had served as acolyte at St. Paul's ten years ago.

The search for witnesses would be stepped up in the morning. But it would be complicated by the marathon. "Sixteen thousand runners," said García glumly. "Plus spectators. Every available cop will be on duty."

"You better get some sleep," Linda told him.

A smile briefly warmed his sad face. "I'll catch a few hours. You two look like you could use some, too."

Back to Queens at three in the morning? Should she ask Mike to go back with her so she didn't have to ride the subway alone? Then what? If he would only stop talking. Bacon and eggs seemed to have energized him.

"He's got to be desperate to have killed Schmidt," Mike said.

"We don't know who killed Schmidt," García reminded him. "We may never know. And we won't know Orsine until we get his service record and a positive identification."

"What are Ricky Foster's chances now?"

García shook his head. "Our only hope is a negative one. We have not found his body. I think my original hunch is right. The disappearance of Ricky is incidental to the murder. He got lost in the shuffle, so to speak."

"You'll show the drawing to Jeanette Ruiz?"

"First thing tomorrow. When we get copies, we'll show it to a thousand people. That face will be everywhere."

"Show it to the shopping bag lady who hangs out in the park. You questioned her, didn't you?"

"Sure did. Got old Lou's usual friendly cooperation—she told the men exactly what they could do to themselves."

"Lou?"

"Her name's Louise. Last name unknown. She goes by Lou."

Linda came to with a start. What was the matter with Mike? He was standing up. He was shouting.

"Her name isn't Billie?"

"I've never heard her called anything but Lou. She's been around the park for years now. She goes away in cold weather, but she comes back in the spring like the swallows to Capistrano."

"My God!" said Mike. "The shopping cart!"

FORTY-THREE

ALARM CLOCKS were going off all over the five boroughs awakening runners.

In his room Orsine tore at the pages of the morning edition. He had picked it up in Times Square during the long, round about route he had taken once he had slipped out of the park. He was sure he had not been seen.

Marathon. Marathon.

Nothing in the paper but the fucking marathon.

Here it was on the inside page. "Park Death Link to Sex Crime?" The facts were few. The victim, sixty-one-year-old Reinhardt Schmidt, minister of the Brooklyn church where Lorna Meyers had been confirmed, had been found dead in Central Park. Strangled. Police were looking for evidence that would connect the two crimes.

Nothing about suspects. Nothing about witnesses. No one had seen a man walking in the park at midnight with the victim. No one had seen him running from the edge of the lake where the body had been found to get lost in the dark of woods and cliffs.

They didn't know.

He'd have to take the chance. Go to St. John's like he planned.

The paper said nothing about Ricky Foster. That meant he was still inside the cathedral.

FORTY-FOUR

THE MEN AND WOMEN who would run the city's largest and most publicized race were assembling in the chilly gray morning light at the Staten Island end of the Verrazano Bridge when Mike and Linda got back to the police station.

"Give me a general impression of the face as you remember it," the artist told her. "Then I'll go over it with you, feature by feature. I'll show you what I've got, and you'll tell me what's like and what's not like. Sometimes it's a very small change—the width of a nose or the angle of an eye. You have to see it. OK?"

Linda was so tired she was afraid she wouldn't be able to remember the face at all. Over and over in the brief sleep she'd had at Mike's apartment, she'd awakened from the same terrible dream. She was in the living room shaking hands with the man who had killed Lorna. Sometimes his face was a grinning skull. Then it was no face at all, nothing but a horrible mask of smooth, naked flesh topped with a thick thatch of black hair. Her hands had reached to claw, to tear—

"Face—square, oval, round?"

"Oval."

"Hair low on his forehead or high?"

"High. His hair was combed back. It emphasized his forehead."

"Eyes—"

When they got to his mouth, Linda had to think. "There's something about his mouth—I can't quite see it."

"Did he smile?"

"His lips twitched. As if he'd started to smile, but stopped."

"No grin?"

"That's right."

"Were his lips full or thin?"

"I really can't describe his mouth." She began to despair How could she put into words the face she had seen so briefly?

"Relax," the artist said. "Just answer my questions. Let me do the work."

An hour later the semblance of the face was on paper. Linda was disappointed. "It's like him, but it's not him."

"It doesn't have to be as exact as a photograph. Your memory of that face is highly subjective. So is another person's. He may look at the picture and say, 'I saw that guy coming out of Gristede's yesterday.'"

But when the copies of the picture had been made, and the police contacted Jeanette Ruiz to show it to her, she said, "No, I've never seen that man. In the park or anywhere else."

Pat and Rowland Foster, their faces gray with strain and sleeplessness, shook their heads.

All available resources were going into the search for the old woman and her cart. But those resources were stretched very thin by the demands of the marathon.

FORTY-FIVE

ORSINE WALKED from Broadway to Amsterdam across 112th Street with the facade of the cathedral before him. In his pocket he jingled subway tokens and his key to his sister's house. He had enough cash in case he had to rent a room somewhere. The cops would be looking at lines in front of money machines.

At Amsterdam he stopped and took a cautious look up and down the avenue. At seven-fifteen in the morning it was almost deserted. The broad steps of the cathedral were empty. The heavy doors had been fastened back. He could see glass inner doors. No one was going in or coming out.

He would be alone on those steps. Conspicuous. Highly visible to whoever was behind that glass door. Maybe a security guard. It could be the same one who had shut him out yesterday. The guard would remember him. Wonder why he was hanging around.

He turned south and walked down the sidewalk. He would have to work up his nerve. At the corner of Cathedral Parkway he stopped for the light. He looked in all directions.

A police car. Down Cathedral Parkway by the curb just before Morningside became Columbus Avenue.

That was too close.

Orsine turned and walked rapidly back toward Broadway.

FORTY-SIX

"WE WENT all through this crummy hellhole Tuesday. What does García think we'll find today that we didn't find then?" The two police officers, who had expected a relatively easy assignment to control the marathon crowd, were prowling with flashlights in hand through empty buildings north and west of Central Park. They had reached one at the corner of Amsterdam and 112th Street.

Rat feet scampered in the dark hall ahead of them. Kevin Keith's flashlight searched the row of doors, most of them gaping off their hinges. The rooms were empty. At the end of the hall, one door was closed. Keith pushed. It gave way.

"God, what a stink!" Keith's partner, Bianca Rizzo, aimed her light at the floor. A plastic jug. A cracked saucer with a congealed puddle of wax. An empty bottle. And a pile of rags.

"Someone's been here."

Keith's foot turned over a wadded lump. "What the shit is that?"

"Right the first time! That's a Pamper."

"What's a Pamper?"

"Disposable diaper. And look—" She stopped and picked up another of the soggy rags. She shook it out. A pair of blue jeans. Very small. Very dirt.

"God Almighty—she *has* been here! I'll call this in to García."

After the message was relayed, the two continued the search—now up the rotten, splintering stairway to the second floor. Another long, dark hallway lined with doors. No old woman. No cart.

In a room at the front of the building a long bundle lay on the floor. Keith nudged it with his foot. It stirred and moved. A sleeping bag. Occupied.

Keith's flashlight found a gray, whiskered face, its eyes screwed up against the glare. "Regular old folks home here."

"Whazza mattuh?"

"On your feet, old fellow. You can't stay here—this building's closed and condemned."

"Fuck, off. Jus' lemme be." The old man's head withdrew into the bag like a turtle going into its shell. The bundle was still.

Keith nudged again, less gently. "Wake up! We're looking for a woman named Lou. Have you seen her?"

The sleeping bag humped and writhed. The whiskery face appeared again and the old man sat up. He awkwardly unzipped the bag a foot. The stench that came from its interior and from his unwashed body made both of them recoil. His hand came out holding a bottle with a couple of inches of whisky left in the bottom. "Breakfast," he said. He took a long swallow, coughed and smacked his lips. "Crazy bitch!" he mumbled.

"Lou? Is that who you're talking about?"

"Lou. Yeah. She crazy. Crazier 'n me."

"She hangs out here, doesn't she? Downstairs?"

"Sometimes she do. Sometimes she don't."

"Where is she now?"

"Gone," said the old man solemnly. The bottle wavered in his hand.

"Gone? Where?"

The last inch of liquid went down the old man's throat. "She done gone to the Lord."

They heard a siren outside, then after a moment, footsteps on the stairs. García came in.

"We can't get much out of him, Sergeant," said Rizzo. "He says the old woman's dead."

"Hey! I didn't say she dead. I say she gone to the Lord."

"What does that mean?"

"I dunno. Never did know what that crazy old bitch was talkin' about. She don't make no sense."

García took over. "When did you see her last?"

"What day's this?"

"Sunday, Sunday morning."

The old man nodded, as if satisfied. "Then I seed her yesterday. Yesterday she go to the Lord. She ain't back yet."

"Did she tell you she was going to see the Lord?"

"Yeah, yeah. Amen. That what she say."

"Where were you when you had this conversation with her?"

"Huh?"

"When she told you where she was going—were you here? In this building?"

The old man paused, considering, his whiskered face screwed up with the difficulty of remembering. Finally he said, "No—not here. We was outside."

"Outside this building?"

"That's what I say—we outside. Down there. On the sidewalk."

"Did she tell you where she was going to find the Lord?"

"No. I don't wanna know. Where he be ain't no place for me!" The man's shoulders shook with silent mirth, and his blackened teeth showed.

García took a step forward. He leaned over to seize the old man by the collar of his worn jacket, but the stench made him pull back. "Make sense!"

"Hey, man, you ain't got no reason to yell at me. These two suckers wake me outta a sound sleep. Now you yellin' at me. Fuck off, will ya?"

"Did you see what direction she took?"

"Who took? What you talkin' about, man?" The red-rimmed eyes peered at García.

"When Lou left you to go to the Lord—did you see which way she went? Uptown or downtown?"

"She didn't go no uptown. Nor downtown neither."

"Then where the hell did she go?"

"She cross the street."

"She crossed Amsterdam?"

"Yeah. That where she go. She cross the street."

"By herself?"

"Old Lou, she always by herself. Her 'n' me. We by ourselves. Got no home, got no—"

"Did she have her cart with her?"

"Cart?"

"The shopping cart she trundles around. You know—wheels, handle? Full of rags?"

"Hey, man, you don't hafta mock me. I knows what a cart is. Sure the old bitch had her cart. And her rags. She don't go nowhere without her cart. She take her cart with her an' go to the Lord."

"Across the street."

"Yeah, across the street."

García left the old man and walked over to the boarded window. He knew what lay across the street from this condemned, neglected building. But he had to see. He tugged at the boards which had been roughly nailed across the empty window frame. Keith hurried to help him. The dry wood split and the board came loose with a tearing sound. It fell to the floor.

García looked across the street to the Cathedral of St. John the Divine.

FORTY-SEVEN

THE GUN had gone off. Sixteen thousand pairs of feet were pounding across the Verrazano Bridge. The front runners were now in Brooklyn.

García showed his shield to an usher and urgently requested words with the cathedral's chief of security.

Nearly eleven o'clock. People were pushing through the swinging glass doors into the narthex, past the huge carved wooden screen and down the aisles. García, waiting for the security chief, looked down the nearly block-long center aisle to the glowing apse at the eastern end. Despair seized him when his eyes swept upward to vault and gallery. With a full team it would take hours to search this place. He didn't have a full team. Besides what he could see, there were chapels on both sides and behind the choir. A gift shop. A museum. Rest rooms. Offices. A basement as large as the building itself. A crypt.

"You wanted to see me, Detective—?" A big man, impeccable in a dark suit and white shirt, spoke with haughty dignity.

"García." He watched the man's mouth drop open when he said, "We think that Ricky Foster is hidden in this building. We want permission to search. Now."

"How did he get in? No one on my staff has reported any intruder!"

"An old woman, a homeless derelict, may have brought him here. In a shopping cart."

"Lou!"

"You know who I mean?"

"My people throw her out of here at least once a week. So she slipped by again!"

"We have no time to speculate how she got in. The child's life is at stake."

"I can't give you permission to search. Only the Dean can do that."

"Then get him for me!"

"He's not available. The procession is forming."

"Hold it up!"

Within minutes the security chief was back. Striding up the aisle ahead of him was a tall, impressive gray-haired man in a white robe with a long, fringed green stole. With every step a heavy pectoral cross bounced against his chest. "Detective García?" he said irritably. "You can't require me to clear the cathedral now. The service is about to begin."

"When will it be over?"

"Twelve-thirty, twelve-forty-five. It depends on the number of communicants."

"Sir, we can't wait. A child is dying."

The Dean looked at him steadily. "Very well. You have permission to search while the service is in progress. Unobtrusively. I want no disturbance of the Celebration. And I impose two conditions."

"Which are?"

"The police who are searching must be in plain clothes. No uniforms. And the other—no guns. This is the Lord's temple. We will not profane it with weapons."

"We'll comply," said García. "We'll begin with the side aisles and the chapels behind the altar—leave the main body of the church and the altar until the service is over."

The Dean looked at his security chief. "Cooperate fully." Then he turned back to García. "We will pray for the successful outcome of your efforts here today." He strode away as the organ broke into a peremptory fanfare.

García looked around again. He had too few men and too many restraints. Very well. He'd have to think like an old woman. She came in with her cart. Ricky was small for his age, his mother had told them, but he would be a heavy load for an old woman to drag up stairs. He'd eliminate the galleries.

The security chief suddenly materialized beside him. "Detective García, one of my men reports that the grounds custodian found a shopping cart on the steps yesterday afternoon after closing hour. He took it back to the trash disposal area."

"Thank you."

She'd carried him in. How far had she gotten with him?

FORTY-EIGHT

IN THE PAUSE between the organ prelude and the beginning of the processional, the organist's glance swept the right side of the choir, reflected in the mirror opposite the organ loft where he perched. He saw what looked like a fold of dark cloth on the green velvet of the front-row bench.

He'd have to remind the choir members not to be careless with their personal belongings. The custodians, too.

The choir of thirty would fit easily into the left side opposite him, where they could see and be seen. On festival days when the choir was double in size, they filled both sides. Then the right side used the mirrors to follow his direction.

Today the mirror reflected only the empty rows of seats below him and that something on the front bench that should not be there.

He rose slightly and craned to see. The thing, except for the irritating token of its presence, remained just beyond his line of vision.

He peered down the length of the wave. What was holding up the procession? They should be in place by now. He plunged into the fanfare that preceded the opening measures of the processional.

FORTY-NINE

ORSINE, DWARFED by the enormous stone pier, huddled against it and tried to make himself invisible. Panic dried his mouth, set his heart to pounding, and made his breath come in shallow gasps.

He'd been a fool to come back. He was trapped here.

He had to come back. Ricky was here. Somewhere. He could not quit until he was sure.

No police cars out in front the second time he approached the cathedral. He went in through the glass doors with people ahead of him and people behind, all hurrying in for the service which began at eleven. All kinds of people. White and black. Young and old. Lots of them were dressed up—suits and ties, fur stoles. But he saw several in jeans. And he wasn't the only one wearing running shoes.

No one paid any attention to him. No sharp look from the usher who shoved a program into his hand. No security guard with eyes fixed on him while he reached for his walkie-talkie.

He'd gained confidence from how easy it had been to slip in, one of a crowd, and taken a seat by a pillar in the dark part of the huge nave, where people sat who seemed to have come to watch rather than to worship. Ahead of him, closer to the altar, the lighted section beyond the transept was almost filled by eleven.

But panic set in again as soon as he had a chance to look around. He'd never find the kid in this place. Even if he waited until the service was over and began a methodical search of every nook and cranny, it would take him hours and hours. Even days. The peace of mind he craved, the relief that would come when he knew for sure that Ricky was dead, was still beyond his reach. He was tired now. The panic would not go away.

The organ boomed and rumbled, filling the huge space with echoes. The procession began. Nothing in his experience at St. Paul's had prepared him for this. A crossbearer, flanked on both sides by acolytes. A robed figure bearing a smoking censer. A choir in red robes. A phalanx of priests in white. One of them was intoning the Introit.

Briefly the spectacle diverted him from his panic. This wasn't a church service, it was a production!

A security guard in uniform was walking down the side aisle. They'd surely be all over the place, keeping an eye on all that gold up there. Candlesticks. Altar vessels. And the cash that would come in when the plate was passed.

The guard ignored him. He clutched his program and took furtive looks to see what other people were doing. No one was looking at him. His panic receded. He could do nothing but watch and wait. He'd be conspicuous if he tried to leave now.

The service began. It went on and on. More chanting. Hymns. Prayers. Prayers for the safe return of Ricky Foster to his grieving parents.

Bullshit!

Mumbo-jumbo about sin and repentance and forgiveness. More bullshit. What did that white-robed faggot know?

His attention was distracted to a bunch of latecomers who were moving down the side aisles. They seemed to be tourists, looking at all of the altars, even going behind them. What was going on? There was a sign outside that said no tours while the service was in progress. Why didn't the security guards do their job?

There. One of them was finally coming up to the person who seemed to be in charge of the tourists. The two stopped by a big pillar in the middle, just before the transept. They talked. It seemed to be OK for these tourists to be wandering around. He wasn't the only one curious about what was going on. He could see heads turned, watching.

The guard went over to the big closed door with the sign Cathedral Gift Shop. He unlocked it. A couple of the visitors went in. The man who was in charge stopped at the door. He turned around, his eyes sweeping the congregation.

Orsine froze. He knew that monkey face. That was García.

Suddenly everything was clear. Not tourists. Cops! They were working their way down the aisles. They'd been watching for him. Somewhere last night he'd slipped up. They'd followed him.

Trapped. Cops ahead and cops behind. No exit except out into the fenced and walled grounds. If he tried to run for it they'd be on him in seconds.

Orsine grabbed the kneeling cushion from under the seat ahead of his. He pulled it out and sank to his knees. He bowed his head and buried his face in his hands.

FIFTY

WHEN THE Dean began to pray for the life of Ricky Foster, Linda's defenses fell. Rage and grief and anguish caught up with her. She began to cry. She cried for her dead sister, for the lost little boy, and for that little boy's parents.

She wept long and silently, thankful that no one could see her. She was alone in her row of chairs. The person closest to her was a solitary man five rows ahead of her in a chair next to a pillar. He, too, seemed to have burdens to bring to the Lord. He'd been kneeling for a long time with his face hidden.

"Don't get in the way!" García had hissed when he saw Linda and Mike come into the cathedral. She'd obeyed. She was so far back in the nave that the white-robed figures at pulpit and lectern and altar seemed to be marionettes pulled by invisible strings from some source high up in the arched vault. The lighted apse with its Romanesque curves and brilliantly colored windows was the backdrop of the stage where the marionettes moved and gestured and spoke.

Mike was as far down in the front as he could get. She'd let him go by himself. She needed to be alone. He needed to be where the story was breaking. What happened here today could be his story, an eyewitness account that could get him back his job.

Identifying Orsine had changed Mike. He was surer, more confident. He was like a man who, having accomplished a goal, sees where he must move next.

She had no hope. The trail of death, from Lorna to Harold Bloor to Pastor Schmidt, could end only with the discovery of one more body, a very small one. She could not see her way, not even to hope that life would have meaning again.

After the prayers she heard nothing. She was surprised when the sermon was over. She took a tissue from her purse and wiped her eyes. The congregation stood for a long, slow hymn.

The unsure voices were lost in the vaulted space. Linda did no
stand. Neither did the man in front of her. Then the choir ros
to sing an anthem. Their trained voices soared. Notes ca
caded over one another, the floating soprano line leaving be
hind a high, thin echo like the cry of a child.

Now the Dean was intoning the Words of Institution. Th
celebration of the Eucharist was beginning. The Dean faced th
congregation and lifted the golden chalice. The organist playe
a mighty fanfare on the trumpet, which the echoes flung bac
in a stream of glorious sound.

"Praise the Lord!" A scarecrow figure rose up in the fro
row of the right side of the choir.

The organ notes faltered and died, and the echoes rumble
away into silence. The Dean lowered the chalice. The choir wer
up on their feet now, craning and staring at the opposite stall
The organist's head popped out of the loft and looked down
Invisible strings jerked all the white-robed marionettes aroun
to see what had profaned the holy moment.

An old woman, filthy and disheveled, with gray hair fallin
over her face. She stumbled out of the choir and into the lighte
space. A long, tattered coat flapped about her ankles. Her fe
flopped in worn sneakers. She waved her arms and screeche
"Lord! Don't leave me behind! Lord, take me with Billie!"

The congregation was up, everyone shocked and staring. Th
nave echoed with murmurs and exclamations. Feet were ru
ning up the aisles. Voices were shouting. Suddenly the stage wa
full of men. Linda saw García. She saw Mike. She saw arm
reaching for the old woman who danced away—back, back u
the shallow stairs to the high altar. García was the first to reac
her. She struck out at him with insane strength.

"Where did you hide him?" García shouted.

"I brought him to the Lord! The Lord has taken him! Prais
the Lord!"

García grabbed her. She wrested her arm away. Other hand
were now on her. She put up such a fight that it took García an
two of the other plainclothes men to bring her down. Lind
could hardly believe that the bony old body had so muc
strength.

"Where did you put him?"

She yanked an arm free from the restraining grip and pointed toward the high altar. Above it the golden cross.

García moved. So did Mike. They lifted the heavy embroidered altar cloth. They went behind the altar. García went down on his knees and disappeared.

When he backed out and got to his feet, he was holding a small, blanket-wrapped bundle.

A cry went up from every throat, a hushed moan that echoed from the farthest reaches of the cathedral.

The old woman wailed, "Billie! Billie!" She sagged to her knees, dragging at the arms that still held her.

Now feet were pounding up the aisles, running the other way. More shouts. "St. Luke's Hospital!" someone cried. "Get the posters!" García yelled. He was running up the aisle with Ricky in his arms. Mike was behind him. When they passed, Linda caught a glimpse of a small white face with closed eyes.

"Billie, Billie." The old woman's wails were louder. "I want to go with Billie." Two men had to almost carry her up the aisle.

Into the stunned silence that fell after the police had gone out the door, the Dean's voice came like a roar of thunder. "Let us pray!" he called.

Chairs rattled and clothing rustled as people pulled out the cushions and went down on their knees. Linda knelt with them. She was awestruck by what had happened, but she had seen that small, still face. How could he still be alive? She would pray for strength and comfort for his parents. At least now they would know.

"We give thee most hearty thanks, O Lord, and we beseech thee in thy infinite mercy to grant life to this child so wondrously found in our midst this day—" When the Dean's prayer came to an end, there were sobs and gasps and murmured "Amens."

The celebration of the Eucharist resumed where it had broken off. So many people, moved by what they had seen, flocked to the altar, that it took a long time to give the bread and wine to all who wanted it.

Linda stayed where she was. She would wait until the ser
vice was over. Then she'd go to the hospital and try to find
Mike. She would know whether Ricky was dead or alive.

The benediction was pronounced. The music ended. People
began to stream out. The man who had been sitting in front o
her in the chair next to the pillar got up. He moved to the side
aisle. His head was bowed when he passed her, but she saw hi
face. Tinted glass with dark eyes that glanced at her. Dark hai
combed back from his forehead.

The face the artist had tried to re-create from the picture i
her mind.

He was here! He'd been here all the time, with his face hid
den in his hands.

Now he was getting away.

Linda got up. She had to stop him! She didn't want to shout
to draw attention to him in this crowd. The man was danger
ous. He might be armed. The police would be outside. The
would spot him. If they didn't, she'd go up to them and poin
him out.

She slipped into the side aisle and joined the stream of de
parting worshippers. At the doors, the streams converged. To
many people were getting between her and the dark head sh
was trying to keep in her sight. She stood on tiptoe. He was jus
going through the glass door. Minutes seemed to pass before
was her turn to get past the crowd and out to the top step wher
she paused to look.

No police cars. Where were the police who should be her
showing that man's picture to the people coming out of th
cathedral? They'd gone. Some to the hospital with García
Some to escort the Fosters to their son's bedside. And the re
on duty in the park where the winner had already crossed th
finish line and those behind him were coming in at 102n
Street.

She was the only one who knew that Lorna's killer was get
ting away.

There he was, descending the steps, moving to the left. Sh
began to run. He was ahead of her, threading his way mor
quickly now through the people who, in twos and threes, wer
moving away from the cathedral steps.

She followed, keeping his head in sight. Somewhere she ould have to find a policeman.

At the corner of 110th Street, he stopped long enough to look ack. He saw her. She could tell, even half a block away, by his ozen stance, that he knew she was following him. He turned d began to run.

Linda screamed. "Stop him! Stop that man!"

FIFTY-ONE

WHEN ORSINE GOT UP from his chair in the cathedral, his knee
were stiff from kneeling and weak from relief. The cops wer
not after him.

They had come to look for Ricky. How the hell had the
known he was here?

He had no time to figure it out. He had to get out of here
He'd go on with his plan just like he'd succeeded. Only now h
didn't have to be in such a hurry. No one had spotted him. He'
go to Barbara's. He'd stay there until they stopped looking fo
the man who killed Reinhardt Schmidt.

The kid was dead. He had to be. That was a dead body Gar
cía had run up the aisle with. That meant he was safe. No on
could connect him with Lorna now. Barbara might be wor
ried, but she'd never suspect him. Schmidt's murder woul
soon be forgotten in the excitement of finding the kid's corpse.

He moved past the pillar and into the side aisle. So man
people smiling, talking, some wiping their eyes. He passed
woman who had been sitting a few rows behind him. She wa
still there. Now she stirred as if to get up, and she raised he
head. She was looking at him.

Linda Meyers.

He ducked his head quick and kept on walking. What th
fuck did it mean that she was here? Maybe she didn't see him
Maybe she didn't recognize him from the other day. He bega
to edge his way faster through the crowd, not like he was run
ning, but trying to put as many people as possible between hin
and Linda Meyers. At the door where the lines funneled dow
to two, he sweated as he waited his turn.

Out onto the steps. Was he going to walk straight into th
arms of the cops? He didn't see any uniforms, but that didn'
mean anything.

He forced himself to an unhurried place down the steps. He must not draw attention. He walked down Amsterdam, moving purposefully ahead of those who were strolling slowly.

At the corner of 110th he couldn't stand it any longer. He had to know if she was following him. He took a quick look. She was there, moving in his direction. There were people between them. An elderly couple, arm in arm. A man with a cane. A frisky poodle on a leash, tugging away from a man in a leather jacket. Some teenage kids, horsing around.

She was half a block away. He could see the pale oval of her face. Now she was close enough for him to see her eyes. They were fixed on him. He could almost feel the intensity of that look. She did know him. She was following him. He began to run. Behind him he heard her scream.

Too late to get lost in Morningside Park. He'd have to run for it, down 110th and hope he made it to Central Park before she set the cops on him. Not as easy as last night. But he might make it. He was glad that he'd been smart enough to wear his running shoes.

He shot a quick glance over his shoulder. She was the corner now, a clutch of people around her. She was pointing.

No cops. Why not? Was it possible she hadn't been able to find one?

One block. Two. He was approaching Frederick Douglass Circle.

Christ! The corner was blue with cops! Blue painted barricades closed off the whole fucking street. How could they have done that—set up a roadblock already? It had only been minutes since she'd screamed.

He slowed down. None of the blue figures lounging by the barricades so much as looked up. What the fuck was going on? It had to be a trap. They were waiting for him to make his move into the park. Then the whole Metropolitan police force would pounce on him.

There. One of the cops was moving. But only to wave traffic away, send cars south on Central Park West. Cars were shut out, but not people. A steady throng moved west along the sidewalk that bordered the park. No cops were stopping them. Ahead he could hear noises. Shouts and cheers.

The marathon! Christ, he'd forgotten about the marathon! The cops had blocked off the street to divert traffic away from the route of the marathon.

That's where all these people were going! Over to Fifth Avenue to watch the runners coming in. Orsine fell in with the crowd. He didn't look at the cops or at the police cars and vans parked by the curb. He'd stay with these people until the crowd thickened. Then he'd slip away from the park and go on over to the East Side and the subway.

Beside him a radio in one of the patrol cars crackled. A cop leaning against the fender suddenly straightened up. He looked at the passing crowd with quickened interest. His eyes fell on Orsine. His hand went to his gun. Linda Meyers had found a cop. They were radioing his description and whereabouts. He moved a little faster.

"You! Stop where you are!"

They were onto him. He took a quick look behind. Two cops, guns ready, were falling in behind him. His safety lay in the crowd. The cops wouldn't dare shoot with all these people around. They'd kill God knows how many bystanders. He broke into a run, dodging the figures that were looking back, screaming and giving way. Still so many of them. The cops wouldn't dare risk a shot. He'd be all right as long as he kept a human wall between himself and those guns. If he could, he'd grab a kid to use as a shield.

He ran on, weaving in and out. Two shots, fired overhead, brought a chorus of screams. Faces looked at him with eyes and mouths open. People were falling to the sidewalk, covering their kids with their bodies.

A cop car was roaring along 110th now, a voice bellowing from a bullhorn. "Get out of the way, you people. That man is a fugitive. He may be armed. Get out of the way. Get your children out of the way. You may get hurt!"

Across the wide space where St. Nicholas and Lenox came together at Central Park North. Should he duck into the park here? No—not enough people on the drive. He'd be an easy target. A family ahead of him, the father trying to pull a double stroller up the curb. He saw brown faces ashen with fear, heard the screams of the children.

Almost to Fifth Avenue. Ahead of him was a solid wall of human flesh. And two cops facing him with guns pointed. They couldn't shoot either for fear of killing someone behind him. He dodged and leaped and hit the human wall. It gave way before him, and his momentum carried him right into the middle of the New York Marathon.

He staggered like a drunken man. He dodged one white-faced, panting runner. Then he hit one and sent him sprawling. He lost his balance, fell heavily to the pavement. The pounding flow of runners parted around him as if he were a rock in a stream. He saw their feet, smelled their sweat. He rolled over, got to his knees. And then he was up.

"Get the fuck out of the way," one runner shouted. Hoarse voices were clamoring at him. Angry faces mouthed at him. He dodged and edged. Now he was at the other side of the stream. He poised himself and pushed. The line of spectators, thinner on this side, gave way. He was on the other side of Fifth Avenue. He ran.

He could hear the confused yells behind him. A couple more shots in the air. Screams. The cops were trying to break through the crowd, disperse them to get a clear shot at him. They were trying to get through the lines of runners now moving steadily in threes and fours, not the superstars who were already across the finish line, but the steady runners who had come all this way and were not going to be stopped. They were coming out of their exhaustion to yell at the cops. Now the crowd was yelling, too. Over the noise the bullhorn kept repeating, "Get out of the way! You must get out of the way!"

Orsine didn't look back. By the time the cops got through the marathon, he would be out of sight.

FIFTY-TWO

MIKE PHONED IN the story to the metropolitan desk. "You're a goddamn hero!" the editor growled when Mike had finished dictating. Behind that growl Mike knew was immense satisfaction.

"Hardly that," Mike said. He was furious that in his eagerness to get the story, he had deserted Linda and run to St. Luke's to be there when the Fosters arrived. He had let Orsine get away. But he knew, now, how committed he was to the job he had thrown away.

"I'm not going to argue with success," said the editor. "You got us a first-hand, first-rate story. Your job's yours if you want it back."

"I want it."

"Good. Stay with the story—the kid, the killer. What's new?"

"On Ricky, nothing. The doctors will say only 'critical but stable.' He's badly dehydrated and he had pneumonia. If the old woman hadn't kept him wrapped in his blanket, he'd be dead from exposure."

"Nothing on the killer—if the man who ran is the killer?"

"Not yet. But he can't hide out forever, and this time the cops and a whole lot of other people got a good look at him."

Mike hung up the phone. The man who had slipped through the marathon had vanished. García's guess was that he had gone underground in the subway system on the East Side. From there he could have gone anywhere.

FIFTY-THREE

"YOU'RE SURE it was the same man?" García asked for the fifth time. "The one who came to your house after the funeral?"

"I'm absolutely certain," said Linda. "After all I did to try to remember him for the artist, I could not be mistaken."

"Surely the fact that he ran like hell shows that he's guilty!" Mike cried. "Otherwise, why would he run from Linda? He recognized her and he knows she can identify him as Orsine."

They were talking in urgent whispers in the visitors' area of the pediatrics unit of St. Luke's Hospital.

"Hold it!" said García. "Don't get too far ahead of the facts. We know he's the man who came to shake hands, but we don't know yet that he's Orsine. We're making assumptions. And whoever he is, what was he doing at St. John's? Did he come to look for Ricky or did he have something to do with hiding him?"

"Maybe he figured it out the same way we did. He must have seen the old woman in the park—"

"You think he killed Pastor Schmidt, don't you?" Linda asked.

"You tell me why he killed his former pastor."

"Maybe Orsine confessed to him that he'd killed Lorna," Mike said.

"Then why did Schmidt go to Central Park, which is way out of his turf? Did Orsine contact him? Or did he get in touch with Orsine? Schmidt had a notebook in his breast pocket. We're going through the phone numbers in it. There's no Orsine listed, but there are numbers with no names. We're calling them."

"When you get his service record—"

"Fucking Army red tape!" García was suddenly savage. "You want to really screw things up? Use a computer! I can't get anyone at Personnel Records today. Maybe tomorrow I can make somebody believe that a killer is getting away while a computer has the weekend off! And of all the unbelievable bad timing—!'' He turned to Linda. ''If it hadn't been for the damn marathon, I could have left men at the cathedral. You wouldn't have been alone.''

Mike realized that his own self-recrimination was nothing compared to the detective's. He had gotten the story of a reporter's wildest dreams, and his job back as well. García had two unsolved murders and a killer on the loose.

''I have to go back to the station,'' said García. He turned away.

''I've got to go with him,'' said Mike to Linda. ''I'm covering the story and I want to be at the police station when the information about Orsine starts to come in. A media horde has gathered outside the hospital. What do you want to do Linda?''

''I want to stay here. I can follow Ricky's progress for you and there's something else I want.''

''What's that?''

''I can see the Fosters when they come in and out of his room. I can give them my sympathy and support.''

''Is it all right if I go with García?''

''Why shouldn't it be? I don't want you to feel you have to be responsible for me, Mike.''

''But I do. You know that.''

''Mike, please—''

''I'm sorry. Whatever you want, Linda.''

He turned to leave her, but her voice came after him. ''Mike, wait—there's something I have to know.''

''What?''

Her words came in a pained rush. ''Do you think that this Orsine—raped—Lorna? Back then, I mean? When she was only twelve? Is that what you think Pastor Schmidt was hiding?''

He nodded. ''It looks that way. We could be mistaken.'' He did not dare reach out to her.

"All right. It's best I know the truth." Her face was white, but her lips trembled and the bruised look around her eyes showed that she had at last been able to cry.

He did touch her then, a light, quick hand on her arm. "I'll be back, Linda. Don't go off by yourself. Promise?"

"I promise."

Mike turned to the elevators where García was waiting.

FIFTY-FOUR

"IF HE LIVES—" Rowland said. He stopped as if the words would not go past the constriction in his throat.

If he lives, Pat echoed silently. The bruised little face and the small still form in the white crib looked as if nothing would ever animate them again.

Ricky was alive, but barely. The week's deprivation had taken its toll. An intravenous needle in his small arm and a tube running into his nose supplied the antibiotics and nutriments that might save him.

Pat could hardly believe the story blurted out to them by the young policewoman who had come to drive them to St. Luke's. An old woman, a shopping bag lady, had picked Ricky up on Monday night after he had wandered away from the place where his baby sitter had been killed.

The old woman had kept him hidden, in her shopping cart by day and in an abandoned building by night. She'd eluded the police searches of the area by keeping on the move. She'd abused the little boy, judging from the welts on his face, and she had not given him food. Last night she had hidden him in the Cathedral of St. John the Divine, where, acting on the clues that pointed the way, García had found him this morning.

"I sat there on a bench in the park with Michael Marlowe and watched that old woman push her cart. Why didn't my heart burn within me?" Pat murmured, more to herself than to Rowland.

Rowland got the words out finally. "I'll never let him out of my sight."

"You have to go to work," she reminded him wearily.

"My mother—"

"Your mother is too old to have full care of him. You know that."

"A professional. I'll hire a registered nurse. A bodyguard. He'll never be alone again."

Poor Rowland. Neither his anger nor his panic had diminished.

She knew that after the first wild joy when they heard he was still alive and the almost simultaneous plunge when they learned how slight were his chances, she had discovered something about herself.

Within her now was a hard core of certainty. She was strong.

She stood up and put her hand lightly on Rowland's shoulder. The tension in him vibrated under her fingers like a current of electricity. Fear and anger were destroying him.

Whatever he had been, he was Ricky's father. She would love Ricky forever, whether he lived or died. Rowland did not know it, but he was heading toward a breakdown. He would need her. They would have to get through guilt, regret, recrimination.

If Ricky lived, they might do it. If he didn't—

She would do what she had to for Rowland, but if he refused healing and refused to forgive, she would do what she had to for herself.

She touched him again, less tentatively. The touch was almost a caress. "I'll be back in a few minutes," she said.

FIFTY-FIVE

HE HAD TO BE SURE.

Ricky first, if he was still alive. Then Linda. She had seen him. She had set the cops on him. He'd never be safe as long as she could look him in the face and say, "That's the man who killed my sister."

Ricky first. If he was still alive.

Then Linda.

FIFTY-SIX

BARBARA D'ONOFRIO slammed the refrigerator door. That fool husband of hers had eaten the leftover steak she'd counted on having for supper. He could've had the decency to tell her.

Bad enough they'd spent most of the day hung up in traffic just because Joe wanted to see the marathon. Why he couldn't stay home and watch it on TV like a sane person, she'd never know. Least he could've done was suggest they stop somewhere on the way home and eat. Now she was going to have to go to the deli.

She reached for a coffee can on a high shelf in the cupboard. She knew it wasn't smart to keep cash in the house, but she had to have some on hand for emergencies. Yesterday she'd put a twenty in here. She opened the can. It was empty.

"Joe! You been inta my household money?"

He bellowed something unintelligible from the bedroom where he was changing clothes.

"I had a twenty here yesterday. It's gone!"

"You musta spent it. You sure came home with a load of stuff."

"That twenty was what I had left! I put it in the coffee can when I got home. And another thing—what about the piece of steak I left in the ice box?"

"What about it?"

"You eat it last night?"

"I didn't touch your goddamn steak! What's the matter with you?"

Barbara looked around her messy kitchen with narrowed eyes. Had a burglar gotten in and helped himself to a steak sandwich? Surely she hadn't left the bread out like that. She went into the living room. The TV was still there. So was the Betamax. He hadn't been after big stuff.

"Joe! I think someone's been here!"

"Anything else missing?"

"Only the twenty and the steak. How about back there?"

"You take my tan jacket to the cleaners?"

"No."

"Come back here, will ya? This place is such a fucking mess I can't tell if anything's gone or not!"

She went back to the bedroom. Her husband was angrily opening and slamming bureau drawers. "Where's my blue sweater?"

Half an hour later, Joe and Barbara D'Onofrio assessed their losses. The burglar had taken, besides the money, the steak, Joe's jacket and the sweater, a shirt, and a pair of Joe's shoes. A visit to the bathroom brought another surprise. Joe's electric razor was gone.

"It's that asshole of a brother of yours. Look—no windows are broken, no locks have been forced. Who else could let himself in? I told ya not to give him a key!"

"Why would it be Bob? He's got clothes. You saw how good he looked when he was here the other night. He's got a razor, too. Didn't he shave off his beard?"

"His beard was so tough he broke it. So he took mine."

"That don't make sense. Bob's got a job. He can buy a razor."

"You gonna report this to the cops?"

"What's the point? Twenty dollars and some old clothes. They'd yawn in my face. I'm really mad about that steak. Now I gotta go out and get something for supper, and you gotta give me the cash."

When Barbara returned from the deli with cold cuts and salads, her husband was in the living room with a can of beer and the Sunday paper they hadn't had time to read.

"Hey," he called. "It says here that somebody knocked off the minister of the church you useta go to. Didn't you say he was here only last night?"

She stopped in the doorway. "Somebody killed Pastor Schmidt?"

"St. Paul's, right? Somebody strangled him."

"Someone who broke into the church? Is that what happened?"

"No. They found him in Central Park. Real early this morning. Cops have no idea what he was doing there. Seems like a pretty dumb thing for him to do—take a walk in Central Park at night. Can't count on angels protecting you there!"

Barbara went out to the kitchen with her bag of groceries. She did not want her husband to see her face. The awful feeling that struck her so suddenly was making her eyes stare and her knees feel wobbly.

Only last night she and Pastor Schmidt had talked. The man had been alive, sitting right there in the living room drinking coffee, and now he was dead.

They'd talked about Bob. About how he always held himself in. How he couldn't have done what that whore said he did, beat her up.

She remembered Bob's dumb, surly misery when he was about seventeen. He was always surly, but that time he was a lot worse. He was so quick on the trigger when Joe kidded him about his lack of success with the opposite sex. How he'd mumbled the name "Lorna" when she asked him why on earth he hung around with those church kids so much younger than him.

Lorna Meyers was dead. So was Pastor Schmidt. And last night Schmidt had come to ask questions about Bob, and she had given him Bob's number.

Why would Bob have any reason to? He might have been crazy about Lorna Meyers when he was in his teens, but he was a grown man now. That whore in Vietnam had lied about Bob. And besides, she was a whore. Bob wouldn't hurt anyone, let alone kill.

She heard Joe grunt as he got up from his chair to turn on the TV. Then, "This is an Eyewitness News Update, sponsored by—"

Joe's yell brought her running. "My God! Look!"

On the screen was an artist's drawing of the face of a man wanted for questioning in the death of Lorna Meyers. A man who had run from the police today and disappeared on the other side of the marathon.

FIFTY-SEVEN

IN THE VISITORS' REST ROOM, Linda splashed cold water on her face. When she emerged from the paper towel, her eyes met a pair of eyes looking at her in the mirror. Eyes in a face so sad, so drawn, that even if she had not seen Pat Foster on television pleading for information about her son, she would have known her.

"I'm Linda Meyers," she said in answer to the unspoken question.

"Forgive me," said Pat with a little gesture of apology. "I didn't mean to stare. You look so much like your sister that I was startled for a moment. I'm sorry for what happened. I liked her very much and so did Ricky."

"How is he?"

"Holding on. That's all they'll say." Her voice was low and uncertain, as if she, too, were just holding on."

"I was in St. John's when they found him."

"You were?" Pat's sad eyes widened. "How did you happen to be there?"

"I went with Mike. Mike Marlowe, the reporter?"

"I know him."

"I was with him when he and Detective García realized that the old woman had taken Ricky. When the police went in to search the cathedral, Mike and I went along."

"There's so much you can tell me. Will you?"

"Of course. I came here hoping to find you."

"We'll go someplace and talk. I'll just stop by the room. If there's no change in Ricky, I'll tell Rowland I'm going to be with you for a while."

They sat in a corner of the empty lounge. Visiting hours were over except for the parents of desperately ill children. Linda guessed that García had arranged for her to be permitted to stay. She told Pat how Mike had stumbled onto the truth—that

Ricky had been taken from the park in old Lou's cart. She described the police search of the abandoned buildings that had turned up the old man and his information that Lou had gone across the street "to the Lord."

Pat wiped her eyes. "Poor old soul! Poor lonely old soul! I should hate her for what she did to him, but I can only feel sorry. What will become of her?"

"The police took her to Bellevue. I suppose she'll end up in an institution. She was in very bad shape when they took her."

Linda did not tell Pat about the man who had run away. There was no need to burden this anxious mother with her own frustration that Lorna's killer had eluded arrest by slipping through the marathon.

"But Linda," said Pat. "You haven't told me why you're here."

"I came to find Mike, and now he's gone to the police station with Detective García. I didn't want to go home by myself, back to that empty apartment. I can't do anything for Lorna. She's gone and I have to get used to that. I thought if I could just see you, tell you how much I hope and pray for Ricky, I'd be able to do something for you. I'm sorry if that doesn't make sense."

Impulsively Pat reached out. The two women hugged each other. "As soon as I read your note, I wanted to know you. I'm glad you're here. You can help me—I have no one I can talk to."

"What about your husband?"

"Rowland can only sit there and stare at Ricky. If Ricky doesn't make it, Rowland will go out of his mind. He may be already. He has to put blame somewhere—on Lorna for taking Ricky to the park, on me for letting her. Poor Rowland! We aren't helping each other. Right now I don't know what to do for him."

"I better stay out of his way. I can only be a reminder."

"No, I want you with me. I need you."

FIFTY-EIGHT

MONDAY. A week since Lorna Meyers was raped and killed. A day since Ricky had been found.

"Alive!" was the black headline over Ricky's face. His story had pushed the winners of the marathon to page two. On page three was the picture the artist had drawn from Linda's memory of the wanted man.

Calls were coming in every hour. He'd been sighted walking on the beach at Coney Island. He had registered at a midtown hotel. He had gotten off the PATH train at Journal Square. Every one of those leads had to be checked out.

The religious aspects of the discovery of Ricky in the Cathedral of St. John the Divine were getting a big play in the media. Every story used the word "miracle." Mike tried to play it down in his story. He knew that deduction and police work had paid off.

But even he had to admit to a sense of awe at the incredible timing—the old woman rising from the choir at the trumpet blast that signaled the raising of the chalice. Then the raising of that small form from its hiding place under the high altar.

On Monday the computer turned up Robert Lawrence Orsine, whose address at the time of his induction had been the same as that of his next of kin, his sister Mrs. Barbara D'Onofrio.

García briefed Mike that evening. "The sister knows something, I'm sure of it. She's nervous as hell. Her husband hulks and glowers. Neither of them will say a word. I gave them the business about being accessories, but they didn't budge. We're watching their house."

García was so tensed up and expectant that Mike began to share his excitement. "They'll break sooner or later."

"That's not all we've got—after I got Orsine's service data I tracked down his former CO. Orsine was given a medical discharge in Vietnam. He beat up a Vietnamese girl, a prostitute, so badly that she had to be hospitalized. She was a whore and she'd taken his money, so there was no attempt at prosecution. But the MPs who were called to the whorehouse reported Orsine as nearly berserk with rage—the woman had suddenly resisted, tried to fight him off, and he'd gone bonkers. The medical report said that combat stress had made him unable to control himself. The Army had taught him to act on his impulses to kill and maim. What I suspect is that Orsine went into the service with a propensity for violence, and his experiences there only aggravated the condition. The prostitute, by the way, was thirteen."

"That's him!" said Mike grimly.

"And," García continued with the air of a man saving the best news for last. "When we went through the phone numbers in Schmidt's book, we found one of them was a seedy SRO on 98th Street near Broadway. We found a room rented to a Robert Orsine. It was a predictably squalid setup—a few clothes, a TV, empty take-out food containers, and a pile of newspapers. Nothing to connect him to Lorna Meyers except one very useful item. Mud."

"Mud?"

"Little chunks of dried mud. Like you get when you bang a pair of muddy shoes over the wastebasket to clean them. The mud came from shoes with deeply grooved soles. Running shoes."

"From the shoes he was wearing Monday? What does that prove? Mud is mud."

"The mud around that comfort station has wood ash in it and minute fragments of broken tile. The lab found both those elements in the mud from Orsine's wastebasket and in the fibers of his blue suit."

"Can you prove the mud came from shoes when you don't have the shoes?"

"Yes, but the shoes would clinch it. Shoes that are heavily worn are absolutely unique to the feet that wear them. Orsine's running shoes, if we could find them, would still have traces of that mud in the fabric."

"Even after he's been wearing them?"

"Even then. If we had the shoes, we could place him at the scene of the crime. Circumstantial evidence that he raped and murdered Lorna Meyers."

"How much can I put in my story?"

"All of it. Keep the public interested. Get them out there looking for him. Tell me—and this is changing the subject—how's Linda holding up?"

"She's OK. She's staying at the hospital, keeping Pat Foster company. They're helping each other."

"I'm glad to know that she's staying with you. I didn't want her going back to Queens alone at night."

"How did you know that?" cried Mike.

"I've got her under close watch. I don't want another Harold Bloor."

"You think she's next on Orsine's list?"

"What would you do if you were Orsine? He knows we've identified him and that we think he killed Schmidt. Schmidt could have linked him to Lorna, to what you think was a sexual experience with him when she was twelve. He may have intended Harold Bloor's death and caused it indirectly. Who else can point to him?"

"Ricky! That's why he was at St. John."

"Who else?"

"Linda," said Mike. "She saw him face to face. She's the person most likely to know what happened when Lorna was twelve. It turns out she didn't know—Lorna never told her—but Orsine doesn't know that. Now that Linda can identify him, he can't take a chance."

"Has Linda guessed about Lorna?"

"Yes. She's too smart not to have figured it out."

"How's she taking it?"

"She's taking it. Her strength awes me."

"Unless we get a confession from Orsine, we may never know what happened. But everything we know about Lorna adds up—a total change of personality, a minister counseling her who was bound to instill guilt, who probably had the hots for her himself if you were reading him right. That explains his attitude about rape and his refusal to tell you the man's name."

"What do you think Orsine will do next?"

"Hide out for a while. Wait till the publicity has died down and he thinks security has been relaxed. As long as Linda's in the hospital, I feel OK about her safety. Orsine would hardly walk right into St. Luke's. Their security is pretty tight. All personnel have photo badges, and visitors have to have passes. I've got a man on the floor outside Ricky's room."

"So we just wait?"

"We just wait."

FIFTY-NINE

JOE D'ONOFRIO stared unseeing at the TV. From time to time he took a swallow from the can of beer beside him, but it gave him no lift. He had a problem.

Rape. An ugly thing for a man to do. Some guys thought it was macho. But he knew he was as macho as they come, and he'd never felt he had to prove it by overpowering and humiliating a woman.

Murder. That was worse. Barbara's brother had raped and killed Lorna Meyers. The cops were sure of it.

He'd never liked Bob. Never trusted him. He'd put up with Bob living with them until he went into the service, but he was glad as hell Bob hadn't come back when he was discharged. A medical discharge, Bob said. Combat fatigue and stress, Bob said. Joe was certain Bob had told Barbara more than he'd told him.

He'd thought there was a violent streak in him, a lot of bottled up anger. Barbara had told him that their dad beat Bob a lot when he was a kid. Maybe that twisted him.

Barbara had made him swear not to tell the cops about the missing clothes. She said they'd never believe Bob had just come in and helped himself. The cops would think they'd given Bob the clothes so he couldn't be identified. They could be arrested as accessories for helping him get away. They hadn't exactly lied to the detective, but they'd come too damn close. No, they hadn't seen Bob or heard from him since Thursday night when he'd dropped in for dinner. No, they had no idea where Bob had been that day or any other day. No, they had no idea where he was now.

It was the next question that bothered him. Had Bob made any attempt to contact them since Saturday night?

Entering a man's house and stealing his clothes—was that contact? Joe shifted uncomfortably in his chair. If a man's brother-in-law had raped and killed, he should be sent up. That simple.

But if Barbara knew he was the one who helped the cops find Bob, the marriage was over. It wasn't worth the hassle. Cops asking questions. Barbara yelling and cursing and packing.

"Joe! You gonna take out the garbage? They come tomorrow."

Since Sunday night when they'd had such a hard time knowing what had been stolen, she had gone on a housecleaning binge.

"You'll have to scrunch down what's in the can to get this in," she said, handing him a brown bag of kitchen debris and decaying leftovers from the refrigerator.

He carried the bag out to the curb where the can awaited tomorrow's collection. It was almost full, but with some rearranging, he could fit this bag in. He shoved to one side the soggy bag of yesterday's garbage. Something underneath it caught his eye. He lifted the bag out to take a good look.

A pair of men's running shoes. They were worn, scuffed, and dirty.

Joe glanced back at the house. She was not at the door, not looking out the window. He rummaged in the can, found a piece of newspaper. Quickly he wrapped the shoes in it. He put yesterday's garbage back in the can, wedged the new bag in beside it, and forced the lid down on the can.

Holding the wrapped shoes close to his body, he hurried into the house. He'd mail these to Detective García at the Central Park police station. Anonymously. With a printed note saying where they were found. Let Barbara think the sanitation men had turned them in to the cops!

SIXTY

ROWLAND FOSTER watched the soft rise and fall of his son['s] chest. Up and down. Still breathing. In and out. Thirty-si[x] hours since he'd been found. He was still alive.

The room was dark except for the light over the crib. [It] seemed to spotlight the unconscious child. All the meaning i[n] Rowland's life was concentrated in the rise and fall of that tin[y] chest.

Thirty-six hours. Their pediatrician, Dr. Grove, had e[x]pressed cautious hope. "This coma should pass into natura[l] sleep, and there will be a gradual return to consciousness. Brie[f] periods at first. We don't know the extent of the psychologic[al] trauma. It is important that one or both of you be here whe[n] he opens his eyes. The assurance that he's safe again with yo[u] will be crucial to his recovery."

Rowland looked at the small, shut face. Did he only imag[-]ine it was taking on a warmer hue, that the rise and fall [of] breath was stronger?

His mind went round and round the same weary treadmill o[f] thoughts. I'll never let anyone take care of you. No one but me[.] Or someone I select after the most rigorous screening. We'[ll] move to the suburbs. I'll fence the yard. I'll drive you t[o] school."

"I'm desperate for some sleep," Pat said, "just for a fe[w] minutes. Linda?"

"I'll stay."

Pat slipped silently through the door which closed behin[d] her. Rowland shifted in his chair. He would not look at th[e] woman who had stayed behind, who sat in a chair on the othe[r] side of the crib as if she had a right to be there, this Lind[a] Meyers, whom Pat had so inexplicably insisted share their vigi[l.]

Pat was leaving him behind. Her new friends were takin[g] over, Linda Meyers and that reporter, Mike Marlowe. And eve[n]

Detective García seemed to want to talk to Pat more than to Rowland.

A nurse tiptoed in. She went through the ritual of taking Ricky's temperature and blood pressure. "His temp's dropping," she whispered. "Down to a hundred and one. Doctor Loeb, one of our residents in pediatrics, is on the floor. Doctor Grove gave permission to pop in and take a look at the little fellow."

Rowland nodded coldly. "Pop in and take a look!" As if the poor little boy was a specimen in a lab. A case study in Deprivation and Abuse, Effects on Children.

He looked at his watch. Eleven o'clock. How long had it been since he'd really slept? Only in brief, unrestful snatches since last Monday. Waking to the awful reality. This morning he'd gone home to shower and change clothes. Then Pat had gone. There was an empty room next door they could nap in, but until Pat left just now, neither of them had used it.

Linda Meyers had offered to sit with Ricky while they both got some rest, but Rowland had refused. Who did she think she was, a member of the family? He knew Pat was getting solace from this woman's presence, and it angered him as much as it baffled him.

Ricky stirred. His little hands flexed, and he took a deeper breath, almost a sigh. Then he relaxed, and the movement of his chest subsided to an even rise and fall. He was coming out of it.

Pretty soon Ricky would open his eyes. He would see his daddy.

Tears stung Rowland's eyes suddenly. He wanted to cry. He wanted to get rid of the iron bands that had been around his head and his chest for so long.

He wanted to sleep. But he couldn't leave Ricky. He had to stay with him, keep him safe. Always.

Rowland's head fell forward on his chest. He jerked it up, forced his eyes open. Mustn't sleep. Must be here for Ricky. Stay awake. Keep Ricky safe. Always.

His head dropped again. Rowland was asleep.

SIXTY-ONE

HE'D GOTTEN THIS FAR. It was now or never.

White coat, stethoscope, ID pinned on upside down, li[
he'd put it on carelessly.

He looked quickly in the men's room mirror. It would ha[
to do. He had to act fast, before the guy in the stall came to an[
started to yell, this Dr. Loeb who'd come in to take a pee.

He'd hidden in a supply closet and seen Pat come out of t[
room where Ricky was. Only the father was there now. He[
have to take a chance. It would be the only one he would get[

There was a cop standing by the nurses' station, talking. N[
doubt trying to pick her up. She was a sexy-looking little thing[

He'd walk past like he owned the place. That was how he[
gotten into the hospital. Security was a joke if you knew h[
to act. Nobody stopped to ask what you were doing if y[
looked like you knew. He'd walked right in with a big crowd [
the start of visiting hours, and while they bunched at the de[
to get their visitors' passes, he walked right by toward the e[
vators.

He opened the door of the men's room. A quick look up an[
down the hall. Then out and past the nurse's station. A car[
less wave when the cop and the nurse flicked their eyes to hi[
briefly.

Open the door to Ricky's room. Real quiet. Step in. Let h[
eyes get used to the semidarkness. There was a light over t[
crib. That was all he needed.

Rowland Foster's head was on his chest. His mouth was ope[
and he was snoring slightly. Asleep! What luck!

He took another soft, noiseless step into the room. The chi[
on the bed stirred, stretched his little arms, and changed pos[
tion. Looked like he was close to waking up.

What the hell? There was someone else in the room. [
woman, sitting by the bed with her back to the door. How coul[

Pat Foster be sitting here? He'd seen her leave. Who the fuck was this?

He took another step.

The woman turned around, looked at him over her shoulder. The light was behind her. He could not see her face. Then he came close enough. His heart seemed to stop beating.

Lorna!

SIXTY-TWO

LINDA'S WATCH had stopped at eleven-thirty. It must be midnight. The hospital was still. Across from her Rowland Foster had relaxed. The muscles of his face were slack, and the tense lines had eased. Poor man. It cost him such an effort to pretend that she wasn't there.

She was glad he was able to sleep. He needed it. Glad, too, that Pat had given up and gone to bed in the room next to this one. Both parents would need all their resources in the next few days when Ricky regained consciousness and needed them.

The small form in the white crib was still sustained by the tubes in his nose and arm. But he was breathing strongly, and every once in a while he moved a little. He would come out of it soon, the pediatrician had said, and come back to the world he had left days ago. They would not know until then what he would remember from his days and nights with Lou. What mental scars he would carry from that pain and terror. And unspoken, but in all their minds was the question—had he witnessed what happened to Lorna?

Rowland was breathing heavily now, almost snoring. Behind her she heard the door open softly. She half-turned, caught a glimpse of white coat and dangling stethoscope. This must be Dr. Loeb. It was too dark to see his face, but she caught the gleam of rimless glasses reflecting the light over Ricky's crib.

He was standing stock-still, staring at her. Then he came a little closer. He was having trouble seeing her face. He must think that she was Pat.

"I'm Linda Meyers," she whispered. "A friend of the family. Mrs. Foster has gone next door to sleep. That's the little boy's father." She nodded toward Rowland, whose head had fallen forward.

The doctor finally moved. "I'll just take a quick look at the little fellow," he said in a husky whisper. His eyes were still on her face. "If you don't mind—"

"Of course not." She got up from her chair and stood aside so he could get closer to the crib.

In that moment Ricky opened his eyes. He was staring at the doctor.

The doctor bent over the crib. He was bald. Totally bald. Not even a fringe of hair. His head was smooth and shiny and tan, like his face. As he leaned over she caught the creak of the starched white coat and its freshly laundered scent.

And something else. Another scent. Faint. Elusive.

She moved to the foot of the crib so she could see his face. The eyes behind the rimless glasses were dark, fastened now on Ricky. His mouth was slightly open, his teeth clenched. Small teeth, oddly childlike for so big a man. Her eyes dropped to the ID badge pinned to the white coat. It was upside down. She could not see the picture.

His eyes met hers. Once. Then she knew. That scent—Lorna's white bottle! The lotion that had tanned a freshly shaved chin—he'd used it again. This time to color a shaved scalp.

She saw hands reaching for Ricky's throat. She saw the little boy's eyes, bewildered, helpless. She tried to scream but all that came out was a harsh whisper. "Rowland! Wake up! It's him."

Rowland's head came up, fell again. He was sunk in sleep, beyond the reach of her voice. She grabbed for one of the white-sleeved arms, for the hand now closing on Ricky's small throat. She screamed and pulled with all her strength. The arm came away, and the other arm did, too, with a blow to the side of her head that sent her flying against the wall.

Pain paralyzed her throat muscles. She gasped, managed to croak, "Rowland! Wake up! He's trying to kill Ricky!"

She lunged to her feet, staggered to the crib and seized the white sleeve again. She could feel the terrible iron muscles, tensed. He shook her off. Rowland was awake, his unfocused eyes trying to make sense of the scene. "What's going on? What are you doing?"

"He's not a doctor! It's him! The man who killed Lorna!"

Awake at last, Rowland hurled himself at Orsine and dragged him backwards off the child. The two were locked in a tug-of-war, thrashing and grasping. She heard their grunts and thumps, the crash and thud of overturned chairs.

The door banged open. The policeman came in. She saw the gun in his hand, heard him yell, "Freeze!"

All she could think was "Ricky!" She leaned over the crib. He was staring with big, terrified eyes in his pinched little face. She put her arms around him and smiled. "It's all right," she said softly. "Ricky, it's all right. Everything's going to be all right now."

SIXTY-THREE

RICKY SMILED WANLY at his mother. Then, snuggled in her arms, he fell into a deep, natural sleep. Rowland Foster stood over his wife and son looking at them with the stunned look of a man who does not believe in miracles seeing one before his eyes.

"Pat—I've been a fool, a monster. Could you—?"

Pat took one arm away from Ricky to reach for Rowland's hand. She held it against her cheek. "It's going to be all right, Rowland. We're going to be all right."

In the hall outside Ricky's room, Rowland tried to thank Linda. He had begun to shake. Words came from him in incoherent bursts—"I went to sleep—I deserted him— He would have been killed right in front of me if you hadn't—" Suddenly Rowland began to cry. He leaned against the wall next to his son's room, put his arms over his face, and sobbed.

Linda stood behind him. She did not touch his heaving shoulders. She said over and over the words she had said to Ricky, Pat's words, too—"It's going to be all right. Everything's going to be all right."

She left him and walked out to the elevator. The hospital floor was quiet now. The bustle and commotion were over. She had not watched the police take Orsine away. She supposed she would have to see him when he came to trial. She would face that when the time came.

It was over. She was so tired. She had thought she would never sleep again, but now her limbs were heavy and her eyes seemed weighed down. She would go home now and sleep. Tomorrow she would see Mike, try to thank him, tell him—

The elevator door opened. Mike. His face was white. "Why am I never here when you need me?" He put his arms around her and she leaned against him.

"Maybe I don't need you," she said, but her face was pressed against his coat and she did not want to pull away.

He was the one who drew back. "Is that true, Linda? If it is, I'll go away. I won't bother you again."

She looked up into his face. "No, Mike, it's not true," she said at last. "But I don't know what is true yet. You'll have to give me time."

"All the time you want."

"I may never be able to be happy again. I could drag you down."

"I'll take my chances."

"I want to go home now."

"Come back to my place. Sleep there again. There's not a lot left of this night."

"No, I have to go back to my own apartment. I have to start getting used to Lorna not being there. Start living my life, whatever it is. I'll be all right."

Mike pressed the elevator button. He put his arm around Linda while they waited. She *would* be all right. He would give her all the time she needed to learn to live with her loss. Then there would be time to give each other what they both needed—comfort, understanding, love . . .

The bond was tenuous now, but it was true. It would grow.

"García wants to talk to you," he said as the elevator opened for them. "He'll have to wait. I'm taking you home—in a taxi. And I'm coming back to get you tomorrow."

THE MAN IN THE GREEN CHEVY

THE HOMICIDE UNIT CONSISTED OF ME AND ANYBODY WHO WASN'T BUSY THAT I COULD BORROW . . .

Chief deputy Milt Kovak of Prophesy County, Oklahoma Sheriff's Department had a rapist and murderer on his hands. To make the whole thing really stink, the victims were little old ladies, the nice cookie-baking, sweater-knitting kind.

His prime witness is Mrs. Laura Johnson— about thirty-five, three kids, an absentee husband—the sexiest woman Milt has ever seen. She's identified a man in a green Chevy emerging from the murder scene. Find that man, he figured, find the killer. . . .

SUSAN ROGERS COOPER